THE BOBBSEY TWINS
AT LONDON TOWER

THE BOBBSEY TWINS BOOKS
By Laura Lee Hope

3/14/61

Happy Birthday
to
Claire.
Hope you enjoy the story!

Aunt Clare,
Uncle Ralph
"Dinky"

Freddie tried to get in step beside a tall soldier

The Bobbsey Twins
At London Tower

By

LAURA LEE HOPE

GROSSET & DUNLAP

Publishers   *New York*

The Bobbsey Twins at London Tower

CONTENTS

THE BOBBSEY TWINS
AT LONDON TOWER

CHAPTER I

A TOY CASTLE

"PLEASE let me saw this piece of wood," Freddie Bobbsey begged his older brother.

"All right," twelve-year-old Bert replied. "There's the pencil mark to follow. And cut the line straight. This is going to be one of the towers for our castle."

Freddie, six and blond, took the saw from Bert. With his left hand he braced the rounded piece of wood against a step of the Bobbseys' back porch. Then he started to saw.

Suddenly another boy called out, "Say, what are you fellows doing?"

Bert and Freddie glanced up to see Danny Rugg, who was about Bert's age but heavier. They did not like Danny much, because he was always making trouble. The boy scowled as he walked toward them.

Freddie continued to saw. "We—ouch!" he cried. The little boy dropped the saw to the ground and popped the thumb of his left hand into his mouth.

"Did you cut yourself?" Bert asked.

"A little."

"Let me see it."

A sawtooth had scraped some skin away from the knuckle, but the cut was not deep.

"It'll be all right," Freddie said. He pulled a handkerchief from his pocket and wrapped it around his thumb.

Danny, not concerned about Freddie's cut, had paid no attention. "Are you making something?" he asked.

"Yes," said Bert, "but it's sort of a secret yet."

"Aw, come on," Danny begged. "Why can't you tell me?"

Just then Flossie and Nan Bobbsey ran into the yard. Blond, tousle-haired Flossie was Freddie's twin. Nan, slim and dark, was Bert's.

"Isn't the dollhouse ready yet?" Flossie asked.

"Shh!" Nan warned, but it was too late. The secret was out!

"Ha!" Danny exclaimed. "So that's it. You fellows are making a dollhouse. Sissies!"

"It's not a dollhouse exactly," Bert said, flushing. "We're making a miniature castle."

"What for?" Danny asked. He picked up several pieces of wood and examined them.

"For the new hospital here in Lakeport," Nan told him.

The money for the hospital had been donated by a man named Castle. The hospital was called Castle Hospital in his honor.

"We're making the toy castle for the children's ward," Nan went on. "The boys and girls can play with it while they're getting better."

"Also," Freddie said proudly, "we're building some small tables and benches for the children."

"Where are the benches?" Danny asked, looking about.

"Over there by the garage," Bert said, pointing. "We just finished one this morning."

Danny strode over to where the newly made bench stood. On it lay Waggo, the Bobbseys' fox terrier.

"Get off, Waggo!" Danny ordered. "I want to try out the bench."

"Be careful!" Nan called out. "It's just for little children. You're too heavy!"

Danny paid no attention to her. Instead, he pushed Waggo off and sat down hard on the bench.

Crack! One of the legs broke off.

"Now see what you've done!" Freddie cried.

Instead of apologizing, the older boy sneered, "It's not much good if it breaks that easy!"

"You meanie!" Nan exclaimed, as Danny ran out of the yard laughing.

"Let him go," Bert said with a sigh. "I can fix it."

After replacing some bent nails, Bert sawed an extra wooden brace for the bench and fitted it into place.

"That's even better," Nan praised him.

"It's bee-yoo-ti-ful!" Flossie said, clapping her chubby hands. "The children can sit on it and play house with the toy castle while they're 'cuperating."

"Re-cuperating," Nan said, smiling.

Freddie finished cutting the last of the four towers, this time without nicking himself. Then Bert and Nan started to nail the pieces of wood together, while Flossie looked on.

"This is going to be a dandy," Bert said, as the castle started to take shape.

It was four feet long and three feet high, but had only three sides. The back of the castle was open to show the rooms.

At that moment, Mr. Bobbsey's car pulled into the driveway.

"Hello, Daddy," the children chorused, and Freddie and Flossie ran to greet their tall, handsome father. He stepped from the car with a shorter man, who had red hair and a broad, beaming face.

"So these are the twins, Dick! I must say they're look-alikes!"

"Children," Mr. Bobbsey said, smiling, "I'd like you to meet my friend, Mr. Baker."

The jolly man shook hands with each one. Then he reached down and picked up Flossie. "This must be the one you call your Fat Fairy."

"And I'm Daddy's Little Fireman," Freddie spoke up.

He had answered to that nickname ever since receiving his first toy fire engine.

Mr. Bobbsey told the twins that Mr. Baker was president of the State Lumber Association and soon would go to London for an international meeting.

The twins knew a lot about lumber because their father owned the largest lumberyard in Lakeport, on the shore of Lake Metoka.

"What a thrilling trip!" Nan remarked.

"Mr. Baker," Bert spoke up, "we're trying to build a miniature English castle."

"It looks like a real one," Mr. Baker said. When the children told him of their plan, he continued, "Too bad it's not the Bobbseys who are going to London instead of me. You'd see plenty of castles there."

He turned to Mr. Bobbsey. "Dick, if I shouldn't be able to take this trip, you're the next man in line."

"Don't worry, you'll go," Mr. Bobbsey said, laughing.

"But if my wife doesn't feel any better—"

"I'm sure she will," Mr. Bobbsey assured his friend.

The twins liked Mr. Baker immediately. Kind-hearted Nan said she hoped he and his wife could make the trip to London. But deep in their hearts all the children wished they might go.

Both Mr. Bobbsey and his friend were so fascinated by the castle that they helped the twins with some of the finishing touches. All the while

Mr. Baker kept the twins amused with stories he had read about England.

"Did you ever hear about the ravens at the Tower of London?" he asked Nan.

"No," she said, as she handed Mr. Baker some more nails.

"Well, a long time ago," he continued, "the big black birds were very common on London streets. They ate the scraps that people dropped. But today there are only a few ravens left, and six of them stay at the Tower of London."

"Why don't they fly away?" Freddie asked.

"Because their wings have been clipped," Mr. Baker told him. "And the birds are carefully guarded too, by a yeoman warder—a Beefeater, you know."

"I'm glad that guard's a Beefeater," Flossie spoke up, " 'cause then he won't eat the poor ravens."

This made the others laugh, and Bert said, "I'll bet they'd be pretty tough eating."

"Those ravens at the Tower of London are not popular with people," Mr. Baker said. "They're noisy and mischievous. They peck the putty from windows and they damage parked cars.

"And just the other day," he went on, "one of those ravens pecked a diamond right out of a lady's ring!"

"What happened to it?" Bert asked. He

stopped fitting one of the castle towers into place.

Mr. Baker said no one knew. Ravens did not usually swallow such things, so it was thought that perhaps Old Blackie, which was the bird's name, had hidden the gem somewhere.

"A mystery!" Flossie said excitedly. "We love mysteries, Mr. Baker."

The Bobbseys were well known for the mysteries and adventures which came their way. Only recently the whole family had flown to the state of Washington, where the twins had had a most unusual *Forest Adventure.*

"Well, I'll tell you all about my London trip when I get back," Mr. Baker said.

He and Mr. Bobbsey went into the house to discuss business. The grownups had hardly stepped inside, when Danny Rugg ran into the yard again. Bert and Nan exchanged glances which said, "What is Danny up to now?"

"I want to help you build your toy castle before it's all finished," Danny said. He took a hammer from Freddie and picked up a few nails lying on the grass. "I'll nail this tower on."

"All right," Bert replied, trying to be friendly. Pointing, he added, "The tower goes on this corner."

"Oh, no," Danny said, "that won't look good. I'm going to put it over here in the middle."

The Bobbseys had made a sketch of the castle

long before they had started to build it, and knew where every piece went.

"Now look, Danny," said Nan firmly, "if you want to help us with the castle, you must do it our way."

Danny scowled. "I'll put the old tower anywhere I want to."

"No, you won't," Bert insisted.

"Do what my brother says," Freddie spoke up bravely.

"Aw, you Bobbseys think you know it all," Danny blurted. "Well, I just won't do anything!"

"That suits me," Bert replied.

With that Danny threw down the hammer, but he held the tower in his hand and started out of the yard.

"Come back with that!" Bert demanded.

"Make me," Danny replied rudely. Then, brushing past Waggo, he kicked at the dog.

Waggo barked sharply and grabbed one of Danny's trouser legs in his teeth.

"Hey, let go!" Danny shouted. He threw the tower at the terrier, crying, "Ow! He bit me!"

"No, he didn't," said Bert sternly as the little dog retreated. "He only nipped your trousers."

"Anyhow, I'll get the dogcatcher after Waggo," Danny threatened, leaving the yard. "Wait and see!"

CHAPTER II

THE TINY TELEVISION

DANNY'S threat alarmed Freddie and Flossie. The little girl bent down and hugged the terrier.

"Nan," she cried, "please don't let Danny tell the dogcatcher about Waggo."

"Don't worry, dear," Nan said, consoling her. "I'm sure he won't."

The younger twins, nevertheless, watched Waggo closely the rest of the afternoon. The dog was content to stay at home and play with the Bobbseys' other dog, Snap, who was larger and had a furry white coat. Snap, who had been a circus dog before coming to live with the Bobbseys, was older now and not as frisky as the younger Waggo.

Shortly after Danny had left, another boy, this one with a smiling face, walked into the Bobbseys' yard. He was Charlie Mason, brown-

10

eyed and good-looking. He was Bert's best friend.

"Boy, that's keen! It's a castle, isn't it?" Charlie asked.

"That's right," Bert replied. "Would you like to help us finish building it?"

"Sure. It's great how you can look right into the rooms."

Charlie held the pieces of wood while Bert nailed them into place. By late afternoon, the castle was finished.

"All it needs now is paint and some furniture," Nan said proudly.

"I passed a hobby shop that's just opened in Lakeport," Charlie said, "and I saw toy furniture in the window as I went by."

"Say, that's an idea," Bert remarked. "Maybe we can go there and buy some for the castle."

By this time, Freddie and Flossie had disappeared into the kitchen. Here Dinah, the cheerful colored woman who had worked for the Bobbsey family as long as the twins could remember, was making a batch of sugar cookies.

As the small twins helped Dinah mix the dough in a big white bowl, Mrs. Bobbsey, slender and pretty, came into the kitchen.

"Dinah," she said, smiling, "when the cookies are finished, don't let these little rascals eat them all. We'll have the cookies for dessert tonight."

"All right, Mis' Bobbsey," Dinah said, flashing a white-toothed smile. "I'll see that we save enough."

At this moment Bert came in and told his mother that he, Nan, and Charlie were going downtown to look at miniature furniture. The three set off on their bicycles.

With Charlie leading the way, they soon came to the business section and stopped at the new hobby store. They parked their bicycles in front of it and went inside. The shop, they learned, was run by an Englishman named Mr. Warwick. He was a tall, slender, middle-aged man, with thinning gray hair, a large nose, and a lean jaw. He spoke in a crisp British accent, saying he was a retired silversmith. One of his specialties was miniature toys. The Bobbseys quickly told him their names and about the castle they had made.

"An English castle, you say?" Mr. Warwick was interested immediately. "That's fine. You'll want miniature armor and furnishings for a throne room, in that case." His eyes danced with enthusiasm.

"Do you have the armor and other things for the throne room?" Nan asked.

"No, I'll have to inquire of a certain shop over in London."

"We know a man who is going to London," Nan told him.

"Then maybe he can find out," Mr. Warwick suggested.

While Nan and the proprietor chatted about the furnishings for the miniature castle, Bert and Charlie looked about the unusual shop. In it were archery sets, all kinds of games, and kits for making everything from toy Conestoga wagons to moon rockets.

"Hey, look at this!" Charlie said, pointing to a small television set no larger than an alarm clock.

"Is this TV real?" Bert asked Mr. Warwick.

"Yes, indeed," the man replied with a smile. "The set was made by my son, Martin, Jr. He hopes to patent it soon. Would you like to see it work?"

"Oh, yes," Bert exclaimed.

Mr. Warwick plugged a small wire into a socket and turned the tiny dials. In a moment the miniature television screen was filled with a scene from a Western show.

"Boy, those are mighty small cowboys." Charlie grinned.

"I've never seen such a small TV in my life!" Nan said.

"Maybe that would be good for the play castle," Charlie remarked.

"Don't be silly," Nan giggled. "They didn't have TV in those days, Charlie."

"Let's see what else we can get on the set," Bert suggested and turned the dial. The screen went blank.

"Oh, oh, now I've done it!" Bert groaned, thinking that he had broken the set.

At first Mr. Warwick frowned as he looked over the miniature TV. He examined one part after another. Then a smile came to his lips. "Nothing serious has happened, Bert. You've merely disconnected the antenna."

This was soon repaired, and the children were fascinated by the tiny pictures which came on.

"Speaking of miniatures," Mr. Warwick said, "have you ever heard of the Queen's Dolls' House?"

"No," Nan said. "Tell us about it, please."

Mr. Warwick said the fascinating exhibit was at Windsor Castle, outside of London. In it was a dolls' house constructed very much like the miniature castle that the Bobbseys had made.

"Many famous craftsmen from all over the British Empire contributed to the Queen's Dolls' House," the Englishman told them. Everything in the tiny house, he said, had been made exactly to scale. "It looks very real," he added.

"Oh," Nan said dreamily, "I hope we can see it some day."

"Perhaps you may," Mr. Warwick said. Then he chuckled. "Something very odd happened

while the Queen's Dolls' House was being trans-
ported to Windsor."

"Did it fall over and break?" Charlie guessed.

"No, not that," came the reply. "A pigeon
swooped down and carried off one of the little
doll figures!"

"Was it ever found?" Nan asked.

"Never," Mr. Warwick replied. "Where the
pigeon carried it, nobody knows. I'll show you
something interesting." He reached beneath the
counter and pulled out a flat box.

When he opened it, Nan gasped. "Oh, how
lovely!" she exclaimed, gazing at a complete set
of miniature table silver—knives, forks, and
spoons.

"I'm very proud of them myself," Mr. Warwick said, smiling. "I made this set while I was
an apprentice to a silversmith. It has been in
many hobby shows. It's not for sale."

After Bert and Nan had looked over all the
miniature furniture which Mr. Warwick had on
display, they purchased a dining room set for
the toy castle.

"It's all we can afford right now," Nan declared. Then she added wistfully, "I do hope we
can save enough to buy that armor and furniture
for the throne room."

They said good-by to the proprietor and
started for home. As soon as the three children

reached the Bobbsey yard, Nan arranged the furniture in the castle.

"Now this room looks lovely, Bert," she said.

"It'll look even better when the castle is painted. Let's do that tomorrow," her twin suggested.

"I'll help," Charlie offered.

The toy castle was the main topic of conversation during supper. A little later in the evening, Mrs. Bobbsey said to Bert, "How about riding down to the store for some ice cream?"

"You don't have to ask me twice, Mother." Bert grinned and rose from his chair.

"May I go with him?" Nan asked.

"Yes, dear."

The two children hurried outside, mounted their bicycles, and started down the street. They headed for an ice cream shop which was a favorite of the twins and many of the neighborhood children. As Bert and Nan parked in front of the place, Bert noticed Danny Rugg's bicycle.

"Oh, oh, our friend's inside," he said.

"Let's stay away from that pest," Nan said.

As the twins entered the shop they saw Danny seated at the counter, licking an ice cream cone. He turned and scowled at them.

"How's your leg, Danny?" Bert asked, grinning. The bully grew red in the face and made no reply.

Bert ordered two cartons of ice cream. The man behind the counter put them in a bag, which he handed to the boy.

"Thank you," Bert said, as he paid for the purchase.

When the twins started out the door, Danny rose. "Wait, I'll ride back with you," he said. "No hard feelings."

Bert and Nan immediately became suspicious, but Bert agreed to let Danny accompany them. "But no monkey business," he added.

Bert held the ice cream in one hand as he and Nan mounted their bicycles and rode off with Danny beside them. They had gone only a block when suddenly Danny cried out:

"Okay, Bert, see how you like this!"

With a sudden spurt of speed, he forged ahead of the twins, then cut directly in front of Bert's bicycle. Danny's rear wheel hit Bert's front wheel and jerked it to one side.

"Hey! What—!" Bert yelled, as he was thrown off balance.

He landed in the street, but held the ice cream in such a way that it was not squashed. Danny sped off, calling over his shoulder, "Now we're even!"

Bert scrambled to his feet and handed the ice cream to his sister.

"Oh Bert, are you all right?" cried Nan.

"Sure, but my bike isn't." Bert looked glumly at the front wheel. It was badly bent. "I can't ride home with this," he said.

Directly across the street was a service station where Mr. Bobbsey often bought gasoline. Bert carried the bike over.

"I had a little—er—accident," he told the proprietor.

The garage man suggested that Bert leave the bicycle there. "I'll have it fixed for you by tomorrow morning," he promised.

"Swell."

The twins continued homeward, Bert trotting beside his sister, who rode her bicycle slowly. A block farther on they came to Mr. Warwick's hobby store, which was closed and dark inside.

The children stopped to peer at the miniature furniture in the window. They were just able to see it from the glow of a street lamp at the corner.

Suddenly Nan grasped her brother's arm.

"Bert!" she whispered. "There's a light inside the shop!"

Bert nodded. He too had seen the light. It was flashing back and forth in the rear of the shop.

"Is—is it a burglar?" Nan asked fearfully.

CHAPTER III

NAN AND BERT, DETECTIVES

"DON'T be frightened, Nan," Bert said. But his own heart was thumping with excitement. "It might only be Mr. Warwick."

As both children peered through the window at the flickering light, Bert rapped sharply on the glass. Instantly the light went out.

"It *is* a burglar!" Nan exclaimed, when no one came to the door.

Bert tried to open it, but the door was locked. "Wait here, Sis," he said and slipped down a driveway to the back of the store.

As he reached the yard, a man came out of the rear door. "Is that you, Mr. Warwick?" Bert called out.

Startled, the man dropped his flashlight. It hit the ground in such a manner that the light was flicked on, sending a beam straight into the man's own face.

He was not Mr. Warwick!

The intruder had a growth of black whiskers and cruel eyes. Under his left arm he carried several packages.

"Stop!" Bert cried, making a lunge for him. Instead, the fellow pushed Bert roughly aside. He dashed up the driveway past Nan and down the street.

"Help! Help!" Bert shouted. Nan took up the warning. "Stop, thief!"

The burglar was agile and speedy. Before Bert and Nan could catch up to him he had turned the corner. By the time they reached it, he had jumped into a car. It sped off.

The twins ran back to the store and around to the rear entrance. The flashlight still lay on the ground. Its light cast an eerie glow on the back of the building.

Nan bent down to pick up the flash, but Bert stopped her. "Don't touch it, Nan," he said. "It has the man's fingerprints on it. That may help the police catch him."

Bert found that the door was unlatched. He groped his way inside the store to the telephone and called the police. A few minutes later, a squad car pulled silently up to the curb in front of the building. Two policemen hopped out. Bert and Nan greeted them.

"Mr. Warwick's store had a burglar in it!"

Nan said and quickly told the story.

After getting a description of the man, one of the police, who said his name was Jim, radioed headquarters. "They'll send out an alarm for the burglar," he told the children.

Bert led the police around to the back of the store. "There's his flashlight," he said. "We didn't touch it."

Jim took a handkerchief from his pocket and put it around the flashlight before he picked it up.

"We'll examine this carefully later," he said, and praised the twins for not touching it.

The children went into the store with the policemen, who found a switch. When the lights came on, they could see that the place was in disarray.

"That burglar must have been searching for something," Jim remarked. "We'd better phone Mr. Warwick and get him down here at once."

He put through a call to the Englishman, and while they were waiting for the proprietor to arrive, Bert and Nan helped the officers search for more clues. They had no luck, however, until Mr. Warwick arrived. Using his key, he entered the front door.

"Oh I say!" he exclaimed, glancing about. "This is dreadful! Whatever has happened?"

Jim asked Bert to tell him the story. "We'd like to know if anything was stolen," Bert said.

Pale and trembling, Mr. Warwick checked his merchandise. Finally he exclaimed, "The miniature silver is missing! And the little television too!"

The owner admitted he had not put these things in his safe before leaving the store.

"I'm so sorry," Nan said kindly. "But Mr. Warwick, don't you think maybe the thief was looking for something else, too? The whole place is upset."

"Possibly," Mr. Warwick agreed. "But I wonder what he could have wanted?"

"We'll stay here and look around some more," Jim said.

Nan thought she and Bert should go home—their parents would worry about their long absence. Mr. Warwick thanked the twins for their quick thinking. Then Bert and Nan said good-by and left the store.

"Gracious!" Mrs. Bobbsey exclaimed, as the children hurried into their house with the ice cream. "Whatever took you so long?"

"A burglary!" Bert said.

"Really?" Freddie piped up.

"Nan and Bert, are you heroes?" Flossie asked admiringly.

While Mrs. Bobbsey served the ice cream, which by now had become very soft, Bert and Nan told of their exciting adventure.

"You are brave children," their father said.

"The miniature silver is missing!" Mr. Warwick exclaimed

"But if you should ever see this thief again, tell Mother or me, or call the police."

Bert now mentioned Danny Rugg and how he had damaged Bert's bicycle.

"He's a real pain," Nan declared.

Her twin chuckled. "But if Danny hadn't made us late, we might never have seen the burglar."

Nan smiled. "And you did make him drop his flashlight with fingerprints on it."

It was not until the next morning that Bert and Nan realized what a good clue they had found. Mr. Warwick phoned the Bobbsey home shortly after breakfast. Nan answered.

"Oh, hello, Mr. Warwick," she said. "Did the police catch the thief?"

The Englishman replied no, but they knew who he was. "His fingerprints were all over the flashlight."

Mr. Warwick told Nan that the fellow apparently had worn gloves while in the store, so his fingerprints were not on anything. But upon leaving the back entrance he had removed the gloves and held the flashlight in his bare hand.

"That's how the police discovered who he is," Mr. Warwick said. "His nickname is Silver Smitty."

Silver Smitty, Mr. Warwick continued, was a world-wide thief. He specialized in fine silver, and stole miniatures whenever possible.

"Then the police will catch him easily," Nan said.

But catching the thief was not so easy. The Bobbseys learned this from the morning newspaper which Dinah brought in from the front porch. There was a long article about the theft and the Bobbseys' part in helping the police. But Silver Smitty had not been found.

"I sure hope that man has left Lakeport," Dinah said. She declared chills were creeping up and down her spine. "I wouldn't want to meet him!"

News of the theft spread quickly. Several of the Bobbseys' friends stopped at the house to offer their congratulations. Blond, pretty Nellie Parks and dark-haired Grace Lavine were among them. Bert and Nan talked to them on the front porch.

"Oh, Nan," said Nellie. "It must be wonderful to be a detective like you."

"Bert, you were awfully brave," Grace declared.

Bert was embarrassed by these words of praise.

He said, "Thanks," then added, "I have to go work on our miniature castle."

He had not gone far when Danny Rugg pedaled up to the front of the house on his bicycle.

"How are the big heroes?" he called out jeeringly. "I hear we don't need a police department in Lakeport anymore, not with the Bobbseys around."

"You're horrid!" Grace called back.

"Yes," Nellie added, "Bert and Nan were very brave."

"They didn't catch the thief, did they?" Danny said with a sneer. "Seems to me you could have grabbed the fellow, Bert."

"I tried to," Bert said, "but—"

"Ha, you couldn't catch a flea," Danny taunted.

Coming around from the back of the house was Freddie Bobbsey. When he heard what Danny said to his brother, he yelled, "You go home, Danny Rugg, and don't bother us."

"It'll take more than a little squirt like you to chase me home," Danny said.

"You're just jealous," Grace chided him, "because you didn't help the police like the Bobbseys did."

"Phooey to the Bobbseys!" Danny said.

These insults were too much for Bert to take, added to last evening's incident with the bicycle. Bert advanced toward the sidewalk. As he did, Danny hopped off and stood waiting, his fists doubled.

"Take that back!" Bert said.

"Make me!"

Bert gave the bully a hard punch. Danny teetered backward and fell against his bicycle.

Crash! Both Danny and the bicycle fell into the street.

"I'll get you for this!" Danny said, picking himself up. He jumped onto his bicycle and pedaled off.

"Fraidy cat!" Freddie yelled, looking up at his big brother with pride.

"Let's forget Danny," Nellie urged. "Show us the castle."

Together the children ran around to the back yard where Flossie was playing. Everyone set to work on the little building.

"I have just the thing for the kitchen—an old-fashioned stove," Grace remarked.

Nellie said she had a set of very old miniature bedroom furniture. The two girls hurried home and returned shortly with the toy pieces.

"Oh, they fit perfectly," Nan said, putting a tiny dresser into place. The two girls then left on an errand for Grace's mother.

Not long afterward Charlie Mason came in. "I'm ready to help you paint, Bert. All set?"

"The castle's finished, Charlie. Now we have to decide on what colors to paint it." He turned to his twin. "What would you suggest, Nan?"

"Gray outside."

"And cream inside," said Flossie.

"All right," Bert agreed. "But I think we ought to paint the outside to look like stone blocks."

"If we do, we'll need some black paint too," Charlie suggested.

"And we'll make the towers red," Freddie piped up.

"Charlie and I will get the paint right now," Bert offered.

"And get some small brushes," Nan reminded them.

Bert and Charlie set off on their bicycles to the local paint store. On their way, they saw Danny Rugg, but the boy gave them a wide berth.

Charlie grinned. "I guess he's had enough for one day!"

Bert purchased four small cans of paint and five brushes. When they reached the Bobbsey house the boys quickly opened the cans and started painting. Mrs. Bobbsey came out on the back porch and called, "Do be careful with the paint, won't you, dears?"

"We will, Mother," Nan replied, smiling. "We promise not to spill any."

"You and Flossie do the inside," Bert suggested. "Okay?"

"Sure," Nan answered.

With quick, deft strokes Nan applied the

cream-colored paint to the walls and ceilings of the little rooms. Even Flossie did very well, getting only a bit of the paint on her fingers.

Meanwhile, the boys were busy on the outside. With the black paint they first outlined the stone blocks.

"Say, this looks keen," Charlie said, applying stroke after stroke of gray paint between the black lines.

Nan and Flossie finished first, and the older girl proposed that she paint the red towers.

"Can I help too?" Flossie asked.

"Of course," Nan said. "Suppose you stir the paint."

Flossie took a flat stick and stirred the red paint round and round. As she did, she pointed, giggling, at Waggo and Snap. They were tugging at either end of a rubber bone. Finally Waggo pulled the bone away from Snap and dashed in circles around the yard.

Snap lumbered along behind the terrier, growling playfully. In his first turn around the yard, Waggo came directly toward the can of red paint.

"Go away!" Flossie warned her pet.

But she had hardly spoken when Waggo knocked over the can, sending red paint flying toward Flossie!

CHAPTER IV

JAM AND JOKES

FLOSSIE'S pretty dress was covered with red paint. Tears came to the little girl's eyes. "Oh!" she wailed. "It'll never come out!"

As she stood perfectly still, the paint dripped from the hem of her dress, down over her knees and streaked her legs to the tops of her socks.

Nan sprang to her sister's aid. First she unbuttoned the dress and had Flossie step out of it. "Bert, quick, get an old cloth," Nan commanded.

Bert hastened to the garage and returned with some cheesecloth. Nan wiped the red paint from Flossie's legs.

By this time Snap had chased Waggo out of the yard. But he returned like a rocket. Both dogs raced right through the puddle of paint. Next, Waggo bounded up the back porch steps!

When Dinah looked out and saw this, she

cried, "Go 'way, you naughty dog!" But Waggo did not realize he was being scolded. He wagged his tail cheerfully and stood there.

"Lawsy me!" Dinah said with a long sigh. "Waggo thinks I got a cookie for him. Bert! Freddie! Come get this painthound before the steps look like fancy linoleum!"

Bert was the first to reach the dog. He took Waggo by the collar and led him off the steps. Then he wiped the paint from his reddened paws. Charlie, meanwhile, had chased Snap away from the house.

The commotion brought Mrs. Bobbsey to the back yard. When she saw what had happened, she stood and stared. Then she asked Dinah to come out.

"Take care of Flossie's dress, please, Dinah, while I help her with a bath," she said.

Mrs. Bobbsey told Bert to go to the basement for a can of turpentine. With this she cleaned the rest of the paint from Flossie's legs. Then she gave the can to Dinah.

"You know, folks," said Dinah, "this could have been worse. That can might have landed right plumb on top o' Flossie's yellow curls!"

Freddie giggled. "Then she'd look like the smokestack of an ocean liner."

This remark made Flossie laugh, and she wiped the tears from her eyes.

"Now for a good bath," Mrs. Bobbsey said, and disappeared upstairs with her small daughter.

Bert, Nan, and Charlie turned their attention to the steps and grass and cleaned up the mess. Snap and Waggo were tied up during the rest of the castle painting job, which was finished by late afternoon. The Bobbseys and Charlie stood back to admire their work.

"The hospital children should love it!" Nan exclaimed.

"How real it looks!" Charlie said, grinning.

Bert thought the paint should be dry enough by the next day for them to deliver the castle. The boys cleaned the brushes, and Nan carried the toy furniture into the house.

"How bee-yoo-ti-ful everything will be!" declared Flossie, who had returned to the yard freshly scrubbed and wearing a pink and white sunsuit.

As it was near suppertime, Charlie left for home. The Bobbsey twins sat on the front porch awaiting their father.

"Here he comes now!" Freddie interrupted, as Mr. Bobbsey's car pulled into the driveway.

"Look!" Bert exclaimed. "Mr. Baker's with Dad."

As the two men got out, the twins raced to meet them.

"The castle's finished. Come see it!" Flossie urged, tugging at her father's arm.

"And we think it looks just like a real English castle," Nan told Mr. Baker.

"It certainly is a beauty," Mr. Bobbsey said, as both men admired the finished job.

Bert noticed that Mr. Baker wore a solemn expression. As the lumberman gazed at the toy castle a faraway look came to his eyes. Suddenly he noticed Bert observing him and said:

"How would you twins like to see a real, honest-to-goodness English castle?"

Conversation ceased abruptly as the twins stared in astonishment at their caller. Nan finally said, "Do you mean—?" She feared to go on in case she might be wrong in her thought.

"Yes, that's what I mean," Mr. Baker continued, his face breaking into a smile. "How would you children like to go to England with your mother and dad?"

At first the twins did not know what to say.

"Is—is Mrs. Baker feeling worse?" Nan finally put the question.

"Not at all," Mr. Baker said brightly, as all six entered the house. "In fact, Mrs. Baker continues to improve. The truth is that I've suddenly been called to South America on a business trip of utmost importance. My wife is going with me."

"That's fine," said Nan, "and it means—"

"It means," Mr. Baker told them, "that your father will be the representative at the lumber conference."

"And take my family with me!" Mr. Bobbsey added.

"Hurray, hurray!" shouted Freddie and Flossie as they entered the living room. The younger twins imprisoned Nan in their arms and swung her back and forth, singing, "London Bridge is falling down!"

"Gracious, what's all the noise about?" asked Mrs. Bobbsey, coming down the stairs.

"We're going to England! To England, Mother!"

Mr. Bobbsey told his wife the whole story, and she was delighted. The family had cousins in England, but Cyril Bobbsey and his family were vacationing in New Zealand at the moment.

"I'll be sorry not to see them," the twins' mother said. Then she added, "How shall we travel, Dick, by ship or plane?"

Mr. Bobbsey said that arrangements had already been made. They would sail aboard the *Ocean Princess.*

Nan was thrilled. "Why, that's one of the largest ships sailing the Atlantic!"

"Oh boy, maybe they'll let me steer it!" Freddie declared.

The others laughed, and Mr. Bobbsey said, "This isn't like our boat on Lake Metoka, Freddie. Nobody is allowed on the bridge but the captain, his junior officers, and the helmsmen."

While they waited for Dinah to announce dinner, the children talked excitedly about the trip. "We can buy more miniature furniture for our castle while we're in London," Nan said.

"May we see the Queen's Dolls' House at Windsor Castle, please?" Flossie asked.

"Indeed yes," Mrs. Bobbsey replied.

"When do we leave, Daddy?" Freddie put in.

His father said that the *Ocean Princess* would sail in three days. This would give the Bobbseys enough time to get ready and go to New York to take the ship.

"We'll have to deliver the miniature castle to the hospital tomorrow," Bert stated, and his father nodded.

At ten o'clock the next morning, Sam Johnson drove up in front of the house with one of Mr. Bobbsey's lumber trucks. Sam, who was Dinah's husband, was a pleasant colored man who wore a broad smile most of the time.

When he stepped down from the truck, Freddie and Flossie scampered to meet him. "May we ride up front with you?" Freddie asked. He grasped Sam's hand and walked along beside him toward the garage.

"All right," Sam answered.

Bert and Nan joined the younger twins and helped Sam carry the castle and benches to the truck. The articles were lifted carefully onto the rear of it.

"Nan and I will sit back here with them," Bert said, "just to be sure they don't fall off."

Flossie and Freddie, meanwhile, had run back into the house to get the toy furniture. Nan had stored it in a brown carton.

"All set?" Sam asked, as the younger twins climbed into the cab beside him.

The truck started off. Sam drove carefully through the center of Lakeport. Teddy Blake, one of Freddie's friends, saw them as they passed a supermarket.

"Hey, Freddie, where are you going?" Teddy called out.

"To the hospital."

"Don't you feel well?"

Freddie chuckled. "Sure. We're all right."

Teddy ran along the sidewalk so he could talk with Freddie. When the truck came to a stop sign, Teddy cupped both hands to his mouth.

"Don't let them keep you there, Freddie!"

"Pooh, they won't do that," Freddie said. "We're going to deliver some toys."

Teddy waved good-by, and the truck rumbled on.

Castle Hospital was located at the opposite edge of town. The handsome white building was set on a knoll overlooking Lake Metoka. Sam drove to the entrance where supplies were delivered.

A man in a white uniform came outside. "Mrs. Bobbsey phoned that you were coming," said the man, who was an orderly. "I'll help you with the castle."

Bert helped Sam and the orderly carry the toy castle into the building, and place it in a freight elevator. Nan and Freddie brought up the rear, carrying the small benches. Flossie had the furniture.

"The children's room is on the fourth floor," the orderly said, as the elevator door slid shut.

A few moments later, it opened again onto a long white corridor. The children followed the orderly along the polished floor to a large room at the end of it.

"This is real 'citing," Flossie said, as she tossed her curls back.

Presently they came to a large door. The orderly opened it and they went inside. The room was large, bright, and sunny. Children were seated at low tables, coloring with crayons in books or playing games. In one corner was a sandbox in which three small children were making a sand castle. Near by sat a nurse at a desk.

She wore a white cap and a starched white uniform. She rose and smiled.

"I'm Miss Grimes," she said. "We think it is just wonderful that you have made these nice gifts for our children here."

"It was fun doing it," Flossie spoke up.

When Sam and Bert and the orderly set the castle on the floor, the youngsters crowded about, their eyes wide with surprise. Several little girls murmured in delight as Nan and Flossie put the furniture in place.

"We're going to get more tables and chairs and other things for the castle when we're in England," Nan announced.

"Yes," Freddie asserted proudly, "we're going to find some throne-room furniture, 'cause this is a castle where the king lived."

As the little patients crowded about, Miss Grimes said to the Bobbseys, "We were just about to have bread and jam and milk. Would you children like some?"

Freddie and Flossie bobbed their heads vigorously, while Bert and Nan said, "Yes, thank you."

Sam excused himself, saying he would wait in the truck for the twins. The orderly, who had left, now returned. He was carrying a large tray of jam sandwiches and paper cups filled with milk.

When everyone was seated, the sandwiches and milk were passed. "Boy, these are good," said Freddie, taking a big bite.

It was so big, in fact, that some of the jam was squashed out and smeared both sides of Freddie's face. As he continued eating, the little boy got more and more jam on his face.

Nan was about to tell him to wipe it off with his napkin when Miss Grimes winked at the others and said, "My goodness, Freddie, you look as if you have the measles."

Freddie Bobbsey's face fell. "Measles?" he said. "Oh, no!"

The little boy looked frightened. "I don't want to stay in the hospital," he said. "Then I won't be able to go to England."

The others looked on, startled. They had never thought for a moment that Freddie would take Miss Grimes's remark seriously. But Freddie flew off the bench, dashed out the door, and raced down the corridor.

"Come back, Freddie, come back!" Nan called out. She ran after him, but could not catch up until she reached the elevator.

"I don't want to stay in the hospital, I don't want to!" Freddie protested.

"Don't be silly," Nan said. "Miss Grimes was only teasing you, Freddie."

"What!"

"Of course. You have a jam face, that's all, not measles."

Taking the napkin which Freddie still clutched in his chubby hand, Nan wiped the red specks from his face. Relieved, the little boy ran back to the table and ate another sandwich.

"Goodness!" Miss Grimes remarked, "I wouldn't keep you from going to England for anything in the world. I hope you will enjoy every minute of your trip, and thanks again for the lovely gifts to Castle Hospital."

The little patients came up to the twins to give their thanks too. Some shook hands, a couple hugged Nan and Flossie. Then the Bobbseys returned to Sam in the truck.

Upon their arrival at home, Mrs. Bobbsey was told about the trip to Castle Hospital and laughed over the jam joke. Then she said, "I have news for you, Bert and Nan."

"What is it, Mother?" Bert asked eagerly.

"It's about Silver Smitty. He got away from Lakeport, the police say, but he was seen in New York City."

"New York!" Nan cried, and Bert added, "Perhaps we can find Silver Smitty there."

Mrs. Bobbsey laughed. "I'm afraid the chances of your finding the thief in so large a place as New York are very small," she told him.

"Anyway," Bert said with determination, "we'll be on the lookout, won't we, Nan?"

There was no more news about Silver Smitty that day. Early the next morning the twins forgot him, because Nellie Parks came with an invitation for all the Bobbsey twins to attend a party that afternoon at her house.

"It's short notice," Nellie said, "but it's a going-away party for you Bobbseys, and lots of your friends are invited."

Freddie and Flossie danced up and down. "Going on a trip is such fun!" Flossie said.

The Bobbseys thanked Nellie and declared

they would be at her house at two o'clock. When
they arrived, several neighborhood children already were racing around in a game of tag. The
twins joined them.

It was not long before all the other guests had
arrived. For an hour they played games and several children, including Flossie, won prizes.

Then Mrs. Parks, a small, pretty woman,
called from the kitchen window.

"Nellie," she said, "ask your little friends to
sit down at the table. We're all ready to eat."

At one side of a border of phlox and zinnias
was a picnic table laden with ice cream, cake,
and soda pop.

Just then a groan came from Bert Bobbsey.
He had spotted Danny Rugg and Jack Westley
coming into the yard.

"Were those two invited?" he asked Nellie.

"No. Mother wanted to avoid trouble," the
girl replied. "But it looks now as if we might
have some anyhow."

Jack Westley, a friend of Danny's, was nearly
as big as Danny, but he avoided Bert whenever
Danny was not at his side.

Jack and Danny looked about. When they
failed to see any grownups, they walked up
boldly to the picnic table.

"We weren't invited," Danny said, "so we decided to crash the party."

"Yes," Jack said. "We won't stay long. We'll just take some of these cup cakes and beat it."

With that, the two boys picked up half a dozen cup cakes and stuffed them inside their shirts.

"Stop that!" Nellie Parks ordered. "If you don't, I'll—"

She ran over to where the garden hose lay coiled beneath the spigot, to which one end was attached. Picking up the nozzle, she ran toward Danny and Jack. Nan followed.

"You put those cakes back!" she demanded.

Nan whispered to her, "If you squirt them, it may start a fight."

"I'm only trying to frighten them," Nellie said in a low voice. "Don't worry."

But Nellie had not reckoned with Freddie Bobbsey. As she pointed the hose at the two boys, Freddie giggled softly. He slipped behind the others until he reached the spigot.

No one was watching him. He put both chubby hands on the handle. It would not turn. With all his might, Freddie twisted the spigot. There was a sudden rush of water. The hose stiffened.

Swoosh! Water rushed from the nozzle directly at Danny and Jack!

"Ow!" both boys cried out.

CHAPTER V

ENGLISH PLAYMATES

FREDDIE'S mischief had caught Danny and Jack by surprise. As the water from the hose squirted all over them, they howled and jumped about.

Nellie was so amazed she nearly dropped the hose. "Who turned that on?" she cried out.

The girl directed the stream away from Danny and Jack and onto the garden. Nan meanwhile raced over to shut off the water.

Danny's and Jack's clothes were soaking wet, and the cupcakes inside their shirts were crumbled and soggy! The other children roared with laughter. Danny and Jack became more angry than ever.

"You'll pay for this!" Danny threatened.

"We will not!" Charlie called. "It serves you right."

45

Danny and Jack ran off, and the others sat down at the table.

The farewell party continued happily. After the guests had eaten the ice cream and cake, Nellie left her place and walked over to Nan. Her hands were behind her back and she said, smiling, "I have a gift for all the Bobbseys."

"What is it?" Flossie begged to know.

"It's for your detective work," Nellie said.

"A fingerprinting kit?" Freddie asked.

Nellie shook her head. "No, it's for examining miniature furniture for the toy castle you built."

"A magnifying glass!" Nan guessed.

"You're right," Nellie replied, as she held the tissue-wrapped package toward her friend.

Nan opened it quickly as the other children crowded around. The gift was a small, but powerful glass.

Bert took the magnifying glass and turned it over in his hands. "This is keen!" he said. "Thanks a lot, Nell."

"It's bee-yoo-ti-ful!" Flossie cried.

"I want a turn," said Freddie. He bent down quickly and stood up holding a black ant on the back of his hand. "Let's try it out right away," he said.

Bert gave his little brother the glass, which he held over the ant. It looked many times its original size.

"That's not an ant, that's a monster!" Freddie chuckled. "Look, everybody!"

After the children had played with the magnifying glass for a while, the party ended. The twins thanked Nellie and Mrs. Parks for their good time and the wonderful gift. Then they started home.

"This magnifying glass reminds me," Nan said, "that we ought to see Mr. Warwick before we sail for London."

"It would be nice to say good-by," Bert agreed.

They stopped at the Englishman's store. Nan showed him the magnifying glass, which he admired greatly.

"You're going to examine the miniature throne-room furniture with this?" he asked.

"Yes," Nan said, "or even find some clues to the things that were stolen from you. Are there any identifying marks on the silver set or the TV?"

"Oh, yes, there is on my miniature television," Mr. Warwick replied.

He explained that his son Martin's initials had been engraved on the underside of the set. "The M is right on top of the W," he declared. "They make a design that looks like two diamonds side by side. You'd really need a magnifying glass to discover it."

Mr. Warwick wished the twins a happy trip abroad and said he was certain they would like the city of London.

"But when you visit the Tower," he added, smiling down at Freddie and Flossie, "be careful that the ravens don't nip your legs." Then he shook hands with the four children.

Next morning all the Bobbseys rose early. It was sailing day! Suitcases were packed, and everyone was ready. As the twins said good-by to Dinah, she dabbed her eyes with the end of her apron. "Safe trip to you all," she said. "I'll sure miss you children."

Sam carried the eight pieces of luggage to one of the lumberyard's smaller trucks which waited at the curb. Mr. Bobbsey would drive his family to the Lakeport railroad station. Sam would pick up the car later.

"Good-by, good-by!" Freddie cried out, waving his hand toward the house as he climbed into the car.

"Where is Flossie?" Mrs. Bobbsey asked, looking around. Everyone was there except the little girl. Then Nan saw her. She was seated under a tree in the yard, hugging Snoop, the cat, and Waggo and Snap.

"Hurry, Flossie!" Nan called.

The little girl scrambled up and ran to take her place in the car. Mr. Bobbsey drove off.

"We're on our way to London Town!" Flossie sang out.

At the station, Sam helped to carry the baggage into the train. Then he stood on the platform smiling and waving as the train pulled out.

"We should be in New York by late afternoon," Mr. Bobbsey told the twins. "I think we'd better go direct to the *Ocean Princess*. It will leave the Hudson River pier at nine this evening."

The twins enjoyed watching the green, rolling countryside and the towns they passed on the way to New York City. But best of all they liked eating dinner in the dining car.

When they arrived in New York, it seemed to the twins as if the towering buildings rose even higher into the sky than when they had been there before. It took two taxicabs to transport the whole family and all their bags to the pier.

"Oh, look, there she is!" Bert exclaimed. "What a beauty!"

The huge ocean liner, which appeared to be as long as a city block, stood majestically in its slip. Two giant smokestacks, tilted toward the stern, were painted red and black. On the bow was the name in bold white letters: *Ocean Princess*.

"Oh, I'm so 'cited!" Flossie said, clutching her mother's hand as she gazed at the crowd of people.

Porters hurried here and there with baggage. The twins watched in fascination while their own luggage was loaded onto a large handcart and put into a freight elevator. The four children skipped up a long flight of stairs ahead of their parents to watch it. The elevator stopped at an upper level of the pier, and the cart was taken out.

"Let's follow our bags," Freddie suggested, hoping to hop aboard the cart.

But at this moment his parents appeared, and Mr. Bobbsey guided the family to the canopied gangway.

"Boy, is this ship big!" Freddie said, glancing around the large lobby.

He had read stories about the *Mayflower* and pirate ships. He had not expected to see walls paneled with polished wood, and thick carpeting on the floors.

"Nearly a thousand people work on this ship," Mr. Bobbsey told the children as they made their way down a long corridor on A Deck. They turned a corner into a smaller corridor and Mr. Bobbsey stopped in front of a door marked: 28.

"Here's our suite," he announced.

A smiling steward dressed in white ushered the family inside. He said his name was Oscar.

"Just press the wall button in your room if you

want me," he said. "That rings a buzzer in my quarters."

There was a narrow hallway with three rooms opening off it. In each room were double bunks.

Freddie scrambled for the top bunk in the boys' cabin. "Please, may I have it, Bert?" he asked.

"Sure," his brother answered. Then he added teasingly, "If the sea gets rough and the ship rolls, you'll have farther to fall than I will."

Freddie thought a moment. "I guess I'll take the lower one after all, Bert," he decided.

Mrs. Bobbsey, meanwhile, found two boxes of flowers in her room. Excitedly she opened them. In one was a corsage of orchids sent to her by Mr. and Mrs. Baker. The other held a dozen red roses with a card: "A fine trip for all the Bobbseys to the land of castles. Martin Warwick."

"How very nice!" Mrs. Bobbsey exclaimed. "Now our trip is really festive."

The steward, Oscar, said that supper was being served in the dining room on D Deck.

"I'm glad," Flossie spoke up, " 'cause I'm hungry."

The Bobbseys walked down the long corridor again and took an elevator into the depths of the giant ship. The twins were awed as they stepped inside the huge, high-ceilinged room.

"How do they ever get so much inside of one ship?" Nan whispered as they were led to a table. On it was a card with the words: *Bobbsey Family.*

Gay and excited chatter filled the dining room. By the time the Bobbseys had finished a delicious meal of roast beef, they heard the ship's whistle give a loud, long roar, then another.

"That means visitors must leave," Mr. Bobbsey said. "We'll sail in a little while. Let's go up on deck and watch."

They took the elevator to the promenade deck. Stewards were calling out, "All ashore that's going ashore!"

On the pier below, people were waving, and paper streamers of all colors were being thrown toward them from the ship.

"This is jolly good fun," said a voice behind Nan. "Would you like these?" Several rolls of paper streamers were pressed into her hand.

"Oh, thank you," Nan said, turning about and seeing a girl of ten. She was accompanied by a boy several years older.

He was Bert's size, but thinner. He had a shock of chestnut-colored hair and his frank, open face was covered with freckles. The girl wore a short bob, and her cheeks were as red as roses.

The lad's pockets were filled with tightly

wound streamers which he gave to Bert, Freddie, and Flossie. As the six children stood beside the rail, they hurled the streamers far below.

"Oh, look at mine go!" Flossie called out.

The great, throaty whistle growled again. The *Ocean Princess* slowly began to slip away from the long pier. People shouted and cheered as several tugboats pushed the liner out into the Hudson River.

"Well, that was a gala send-off," Mrs. Bobbsey remarked. She smiled at the two children who stood beside her twins.

"We're the Bobbseys," Nan said, and introduced her family.

"And we're the Radfords," said the girl. "I'm Gail, and this is my brother, Gavin."

"Judging from your accent, I'd say you're British," Mr. Bobbsey remarked, smiling.

Gail and Gavin said yes, they were. They and their parents had been to America on a tour and were now returning to London.

"That's where we're going!" Freddie spoke up.

"Then we can show you around London a bit when we arrive there," Gail offered.

"Great!" said Bert. "Have you ever been on the *Ocean Princess* before?" he asked.

The Radford children replied no, whereupon Bert added, "Then let's explore her tomorrow."

"Righto," Gavin agreed. "That would be jolly. We'll meet here on the deck after breakfast. Cheerio." They went off.

The twins remained near the railing while the *Ocean Princess* steamed through the Narrows and out to sea. By this time it was dark. Lights blinked along the shore of New Jersey and Long Island. At last the children returned to Cabin 28 and quickly climbed into their bunks.

Next morning, Freddie was first to awaken. He hurried over to the porthole and looked out.

"Bert!" he cried. "Look! There's nothing but water."

Aroused, Bert took in the magnificent view of the Atlantic. The greenish water rolled gently in the sparkling sunshine.

On the way to breakfast Freddie and Flossie discovered a children's playroom, gaily decorated and filled with games and toys. They decided to come back here instead of going with Gail and Gavin.

After Bert and Nan had had orange juice, oatmeal, and boiled eggs, they hurried to the promenade deck. "Hi!" the twins called, seeing their new friends.

"Hi!" the Radfords replied in their British accent, and Gail added, "Come on, let's explore."

The four children set off around the promenade deck. Then they climbed up an outside stairway to the boat deck.

"Neat," said Bert as they gazed at the giant lifeboats with gasoline motors. The boats were arranged on davits on either side of the ocean liner, ready to be swung down into the water if necessary.

After exploring the boat deck, Gavin descended the iron steps. Just as Nan started to follow him, the ship gave a lurch. She lost her balance.

"Look out!" Bert cried.

Nan would have pitched down the stairs. But Gavin, hearing the warning, turned quickly and caught her.

"Thanks a million," Nan said.

Gavin grinned. "I say, we must have gone over a whale!"

When they reached the lower deck, Gail said, "Nan, I know something you'd like to see." She told her American friend about the lovely shops on the ship. "I'll show you the dolls!"

Gavin and Bert ambled off toward the bow of the ship to watch a group of seamen coiling thick hawsers. Gail and Nan walked down to C Deck, where the shops were located. In one tiny shop was the collection of lovely French, English, and Dutch dolls.

"Oh, they're sweet!" Nan exclaimed. "I hope I can buy one on the return trip. We're coming back on this same ship."

Next door Gail pointed out a beautiful display of Danish silver. Spoons, pitchers, bowls, and many other pieces were exquisite in design, with hand-scrolled work. Also on sale were French perfumes, Scottish plaid blankets, and attractive Parisian blouses.

"Yummy!" said Nan.

Gail giggled. "We'd say, 'A bit of all right.' "

As the girls walked out of the shop, Bert and Gavin hurried up to them. "Let's go to the swimming pool," Bert said. "Freddie and Flossie are already in it."

"Oh, yes," both girls agreed.

The playmates separated, promising to meet

at the pool in ten minutes. Bert and Nan made their way to the Bobbsey suite. As they walked through the long corridor, the ship began to roll.

"The sea must be getting rougher," Nan remarked, as she held out her hands to keep from bumping against the sides of the long passageway.

Entering their staterooms, the twins found their bathing suits. Then they hurried to the pool, which was located half a floor below the restaurant on D Deck. Freddie and Flossie, along with Mr. and Mrs. Bobbsey, were splashing about gaily in the large salt-water tank.

"Right this way," an attendant said, smiling. "But hurry. We may have to close the pool if the ocean gets any rougher."

He showed the twins to the men's and women's locker rooms, where they were joined by Gail and Gavin. A few minutes later they all dived into the pool.

"This is just like swimming in the ocean," Bert said, as the waves slapped back and forth with the rocking of the ship.

They had been in the water no longer than five minutes before the attendant called out:

"It's getting too rough. Everybody out, please."

Flossie, however, was reluctant to leave the pool. The little girl, who swam well, tarried while the others climbed out before her. Then suddenly—*swish! smack!* The ship rolled over so far that a giant wave was formed in the small pool. Flossie was carried up on the crest of it.

"Oh!" Mrs. Bobbsey cried out, as the wave sloshed over the side of the pool, carrying Flossie onto the tile apron which circled the tank.

Bang! She sprawled on the hard surface.

"Oomp!" Flossie gurgled. The wind had been knocked from her.

The attendant and Mr. Bobbsey ran to the little girl's side. "Are you hurt, dear?" her father asked anxiously, picking up his small daughter.

Flossie gasped a few times until she caught her breath. "I'm—I'm all right, Daddy," she said finally. Then she grinned. "I never heard of ocean waves inside of a ship before!"

This remark made the others laugh, and they knew the little girl was all right. During the rough weather the Bobbseys stayed in their cabin. But by lunchtime the ocean was calm again. The meal over, the children played shuffleboard and Ping Pong on deck. Then in the late afternoon they joined their parents in deck chairs with a blanket thrown over them against the chill wind. All of them fell asleep in the balmy, salty air!

Next day startling news greeted them at the

breakfast table. The passengers were buzzing excitedly.

"Have you heard the news?" a woman at a near-by table asked. She leaned over to Mrs. Bobbsey.

"No. What happened?"

"The silver shop was robbed. Some lovely Danish silver was taken. Can you imagine? We have a thief on board!"

Nan's eyes widened. "Oh, Mother," she said, "do you suppose Silver Smitty is on the *Ocean Princess?*"

CHAPTER VI

MYSTERY AT SEA

"SILVER SMITTY, did you say?" asked a ship's officer who was walking past their table. He was a short, stocky man wearing captain's bars. He introduced himself as Captain Taylor. "What do you know about Silver Smitty?"

At Mr. Bobbsey's suggestion Bert supplied the answer. He told Captain Taylor of the twins' adventure at Mr. Warwick's store. "Later we heard that Silver Smitty was seen in New York City," Bert added.

"Maybe he's on the ship in disguise," Freddie spoke up.

"Possibly," Captain Taylor said. "Whoever the thief is, he is clever." He told how the burglar had cut a piece out of the shopwindow and had reached in to take the silver. "We're searching the entire vessel now," the captain added.

"Do you mind if we look for Silver Smitty?" Nan asked him.

"No, I don't mind," Captain Taylor replied. "But don't do anything dangerous."

"We won't," Nan promised.

On and off during the rest of the day the younger twins walked about with their mother. Bert and Nan, meanwhile, with Gail and Gavin Radford, strolled about the decks studying the passengers. Many of them were reclining in deck chairs. The men had caps pulled low over their eyes, and nearly everyone wore sun glasses.

"I wish we could get a better look at these people," Bert remarked to Gavin. "Especially that man with the brown beard."

"I'd love to tug it." Gavin grinned. "Just to make sure it's real."

Bert chuckled. "I'm afraid if we tugged at it, we'd get in trouble," he said.

The twins stopped hunting for Silver Smitty for a while during the afternoon to take a swim in the pool. But after supper Bert left the others to stroll about the dark decks once more.

Bert's meandering finally took him to the boat deck. He strolled along close to the cabin wall of the ship. Suddenly, in the gloom ahead of him, he saw a man step out cautiously from behind a stairway and move forward.

Bert dropped down beside a deck chair and

peered over it, his heart thumping wildly. There was something familiar about the fellow. His build and walk reminded the boy of the thief who had dashed out of the shop in Lakeport!

"I wonder if it could be—" he asked himself excitedly as his eyes followed the dim figure.

Bert crept from his hiding place. Pressing close to the wall of the cabin, he inched forward. Then he stopped again.

In the semi-darkness he saw the man squeeze under the tarpaulin of one of the lifeboats. Bert ventured closer and could see that one of the ropes had been slashed. He wanted to call out an alarm, but there was no one else in sight.

The man was about to reach under one of the seats of the lifeboat when suddenly he turned about. Bert knew the man had seen him. The boy was about to yell for help when suddenly a chair rug was tossed over his head.

"Help!" Bert shouted. But his cries were muffled by the rug which was drawn tightly over him.

"The fellow must have a helper," Bert thought as he struggled to free himself.

Rough hands, however, encircled the boy, holding him tight. Then as suddenly as he had been attacked, Bert felt himself released. He thrashed about, finally throwing the rug off his head. Dazed, the boy stood still and gazed

He saw a man squeeze under the tarpaulin

around. No one was in sight. The lifeboat was empty.

With the speed of a deer, Bert ran along the deck and dashed down a stairway. He almost bumped into one of the ship's officers.

"I must see Captain Taylor at once," Bert said, panting. "I think I saw the thief!"

He explained what had happened and was taken at once to the captain's quarters.

"You think you saw the thief? Where?" the ruddy-complexioned Britisher asked.

Bert told of his experience. The captain quickly called in the ship's detective, a tall man with a sharp nose.

"Mr. Fagan," the captain said as he introduced Bert, "this lad thinks Silver Smitty is aboard and that he saw him. Tell Mr. Fagan how you were attacked, Bert."

Again Bert gave the information. Then all three hurried to the boat deck.

"There's where I saw him," Bert said, pointing.

The detective climbed under the tarpaulin and with a flashlight searched the lifeboat thoroughly.

"I say now, what's this?" he murmured, picking up something from the bottom of the boat. Climbing nimbly out again, he showed it to Captain Taylor and Bert.

"A small knob for some sort of a contraption," Captain Taylor said, examining the object in the palm of his hand.

"I think I know what it is," Bert said eagerly. "It's a knob from a tiny television set which was stolen by Silver Smitty in Lakeport, where I live."

"It begins to look," said Mr. Fagan, "as if this clever thief *is* aboard, Captain Taylor."

"We must take every means to find him," the captain declared. "One thing is certain. He can't get off the ship!"

Mr. Fagan said he would keep the knob as evidence, but later Bert might have it to return to Mr. Warwick. "I hope we'll find the rest of the miniature TV set," the detective added.

Bert hoped so too, and further wished that he might be the one to find it.

When Bert told his family what had happened, his parents were alarmed.

"Oh dear," Mrs. Bobbsey said nervously. "I hope they catch that man and his partner soon."

"And Bert," his father added sternly, "don't go off by yourself again."

Next morning the ship's daily newspaper contained an item about the theft of the Danish silver, but did not mention Bert's adventure. There was another article, however, which did speak of the Bobbsey twins and their miniature castle.

"I'll bet Gail and Gavin told the reporters about this," Bert said, grinning.

They saw their English playmates having breakfast in the dining room with their parents. After the grownups were introduced by the children, Mrs. Radford, a small woman with a beautiful English complexion, declared that the Bobbsey twins were about to enjoy a surprise.

"What is it?" Flossie wanted to know.

Mrs. Radford looked at her husband, a tall, athletic-looking man with a bristly brown mustache. "Mr. Radford and I promised to keep it a secret," she said, "unless Gail and Gavin wish to tell you."

But the English children said nothing. Instead they grinned broadly, and Gavin remarked, "You wait and see. But it's jolly good. You'll know about it tomorrow."

The twins did not see much of Gail and Gavin the rest of that day. Once Nan noticed Gail talking to a woman on the deck who opened her handbag and gave the girl something. When Gail saw Nan, she hurried off in another direction.

"Say, what are they up to?" Bert said at dinner that evening. "Gavin has been avoiding me all day."

"I'm sure it's not because he doesn't like you," Mrs. Bobbsey said reassuringly.

"Maybe it's part of their surprise," Nan guessed. "I just can't wait to find out what it is."

After dinner the Bobbseys entered the large and beautifully furnished salon where musicians were playing soft, sweet melodies.

"Oh, there you are," Gavin Radford said, walking over to them.

His sister followed. "We have a surprise for you," she announced, beaming. Reaching into her pocket, Gail pulled out a white envelope and handed it to Nan. "Please open it."

Puzzled, Nan lifted the flap and looked inside. The envelope was filled with crisp English pound notes.

"Money!" Freddie cried out. "For us?"

Gavin said it was a collection that he and Gail had taken up on the ship, and it was equal to a hundred American dollars.

"It's for miniature furniture to put in the children's castle at the hospital," Gavin said.

"How marvelous!" Nan exclaimed.

Mrs. Bobbsey said the passengers aboard the *Ocean Princess* were certainly generous and the Radford children most thoughtful.

"You're a dear!" Nan said, kissing Gail.

Bert wrung Gavin's hand. "Oh boy!" he declared. "Now we'll be able to buy real throne-room furniture. Won't those kids in Castle Hospital love it!"

As the Bobbseys were about to retire for the night, the telephone rang in Mr. Bobbsey's stateroom. Captain Taylor was calling. He reported that no trace of Silver Smitty or any other thief had been found. A radio message to the New York police had revealed, however, that Silver Smitty had been seen near the waterfront several days before.

"This seems to bear out your son's hunch that the man may be aboard our ship," the officer said. "We'll continue our search."

But the following day, when Bert and Nan talked to Detective Fagan on deck, he said, "We have no clue yet to the thief."

"How about the crew?" Bert asked. "Have you checked them?"

"Oh, yes. It appears that none of them is the culprit. Our only hope now is that the thief will come out of hiding when the ship docks at Southampton tomorrow. All baggage will be opened at customs and carefully inspected. Also, if anyone tries to sneak ashore, he'll be caught."

The twins continued to talk about this all during the evening. Early next morning they lined up with Gail and Gavin and other passengers at the railing to catch their first glimpse of land. The *Ocean Princess* was still a half hour out from Southampton. Suddenly a cry came from someone on the deck above them.

"Man overboard!"

Bert and Nan felt the big liner shudder as the motors were thrown into reverse. Then they saw a man in the water thirty feet off the starboard bow.

"Will he drown?" Flossie cried out in alarm.

"No, honey. He's swimming," Nan replied.

Several crewmen of the *Ocean Princess* began to lower one of the lifeboats. Just then Bert noticed an oilskin package floating in the water next to the swimmer. It apparently was tied to his body, and he seemed to be heading toward shore.

Just then the high-pitched sound of a fast motorboat reached the twins' ears. "It's a speedboat!" Freddie cried out.

At this moment the lifeboat of the *Ocean Princess* touched the water. The crew started the motor and headed toward the swimmer. But the speedboat reached the man first. He threw the oilskin package into the boat and clambered aboard.

A crewman from the lifeboat called for him to halt. Instead, the cream and gold-colored speedboat turned about and raced back toward shore.

"It's the thief! He's escaping!" Bert yelled.

CHAPTER VII

THE PICKLE CIRCUS

PASSENGERS who heard Bert agreed with the boy. The man who had jumped overboard was indeed the thief. He had taken the stolen Danish silver with him!

"And the miniatures and the tiny TV set," Nan whispered to her family.

"He is very daring," Mrs. Bobbsey said. "He'll be hard to capture now."

At this moment Detective Fagan came up to the Bobbseys and admitted the thief had outwitted them. "We've wirelessed the shore police. But I'm afraid the speedboat will land in some out-of-the-way spot and Silver Smitty will run away before they get there."

"You mean Mr. Warwick will never get his 'mintures' back?" Flossie asked.

"I wouldn't say that, lass," Mr. Fagan answered. "He'll like as not turn up in London, and some bobby will arrest him."

"Who's Bobby?" Freddie spoke up.

The detective laughed and told the twins that policemen in London were called bobbies. They were so named in honor of Robert Peel, called Bobby, who had set up the London police department more than a hundred years before.

Mr. Fagan went on to tell the Bobbseys more about Silver Smitty. The detective had learned from the authorities that the thief was an American who once had lived in London.

"Was he an honest man then?" Nan asked.

"No," Mr. Fagan replied. "Silver Smitty was jailed for theft in London, but managed to flee to America."

"Why is he returning to England now?" Bert wondered aloud. But Mr. Fagan could not answer this and now said, "Well, cheerio, children. And good luck!" He moved off.

When the ship docked, Gail, Gavin, and their parents said good-by to the Bobbseys. "We live in the outskirts of London," Mrs. Radford added. "You must come to visit us."

"I'd love to," said Nan. "But can't you visit us first at our hotel?"

"We'll try to arrange it," Mr. Radford replied.

"We'll be staying at the Park Hotel on Piccadilly," Mrs. Bobbsey said, "directly across the street from Green Park."

"We'll be seeing you!" the children called to one another as they parted on the dock.

After going through customs, the passengers boarded the boat train. Several hours later they found themselves in London. What a busy place it was! The Bobbseys took a cab and drove through the streets of the lovely city.

"Isn't it quaint?" Nan said as she looked at the interesting old buildings. "It looks like pictures on Christmas cards."

"And all the cars are little, and they're driving on the wrong side of the street," Freddie said.

Hearing this, the cabby smiled and looked back over his shoulder. "That's the way we get about in England, lad." Then he warned the children to be careful crossing the streets. "Instead of looking to your left as you do in your country," he said, "look to the right to be sure no cars are coming."

As the twins nodded, Freddie exclaimed, "Look at the funny hat on that man!"

A tall man was striding along vigorously. In his right hand he swung a cane, and on his head sat a bowler hat.

"He's probably a barrister," the cabby explained with a grin.

"A what?" Bert asked.

"A lawyer," the driver explained.

"Oh, England is such fun already," Flossie said, clapping her hands.

Soon the cab pulled up in front of their hotel. It stood back from a broad sidewalk. The Bobbseys got out and entered the expansive lobby. People were seated about small tables drinking tea and eating pastries.

"English teatime," Mrs. Bobbsey remarked as they made their way to the rear of the lobby.

Mr. Bobbsey signed the register and told the hall porter that their baggage would arrive soon.

"We'll bring it to your rooms directly, sir," the hall porter replied. "Please take the lift over there."

He called a boy who directed the Bobbseys to their three-room suite on the third floor. As he opened the windows, he said, "It's only a bit of a walk to Piccadilly Circus. You'll want to see that."

The baggage arrived shortly. Mr. and Mrs. Bobbsey, and Bert and Nan unpacked the suitcases.

"May Freddie and I go out in the hall and look around?" Flossie asked. "I hear some children."

"All right, but come back soon," their mother said.

The twins found that the children were on their way downstairs to get crumpets and tea.

"Let's go find out what crumpets are," Freddie suggested. "They must be something to eat."

The twins followed the others down a stairway to the lobby. They sat down at a small table. A moment later a waitress with a black dress and saucy-looking white cap came to ask them what they wanted.

"Crumpets and tea," said Freddie manfully.

The waitress smiled as she went off. In a few moments she returned with cups of tea in which there was a great deal of milk. She also set down a plate full of small, flat cakes.

Freddie bit into one. "Good," he said.

Flossie sipped her tea. "This is real sweet and good."

The waitress now laid the bill for the refreshments on the table. The twins looked worried. They had thought the tea and crumpets were free!

"We—we haven't any money," said Freddie, on the verge of tears.

The young woman smiled. "Just sign your name. Your papa can pay for it later." Freddie wrote his name.

When the twins finished eating, Flossie remarked, "What do you suppose the pickle circus looks like?"

"Let's find out," Freddie proposed. "It won't take long."

Hand in hand, they went through the revolving door and Freddie asked the doorman, "Where's the circus, please, sir?"

"Go to your left," the man said, smiling. "You can't miss it."

Freddie and Flossie made their way down the broad sidewalk. The small, black taxis whizzing by fascinated them, as did the double-decker buses. Presently they came to a large circular area. In the middle of it was a tall shaft. On top was the statue of a boy with a bow and arrow. Streets ran out like the spokes of a wheel from the circle.

"I don't see any circus," Freddie complained as he looked about.

"Let's ask someone," Flossie suggested. She tugged her brother's hand and pointed. "Look, there's a Robert!" she said.

"You mean the man in the uniform?" Freddie asked.

"Yes. He can tell us where the circus is."

The children watched the light on the street corner change. Then they hurried across and walked up to the uniformed man.

"Are you a Robert?" Flossie asked him.

The officer, a young man with a tall, bowler-shaped hat, smiled down at the twins. "You mean a bobby?"

"That's it!" Flossie said.

"Yes, I'm a bobby. I guess you'd call me a policeman. What can I do for you little Americans?"

"We're looking for the circus," Freddie said, "because we want to see the elephants."

"Circus? Elephants?" The bobby looked puzzled.

"Yes. We heard the pickle circus was near here," Freddie said. "Do the clowns in it eat pickles?"

Now the bobby burst into laughter. "You mean Piccadilly Circus!" he said.

"That's it," Flossie added. "Where's the Piccadilly Circus?"

"Right here. You're looking at it," the bobby told her.

Freddie and Flossie looked about, bewildered. They had expected to see tents and peanut vendors and cotton candy. Instead, what they saw was a large traffic circle with cars whizzing around it.

The officer bent down with an arm around each of the twins and explained to them that in London a circus merely means a circular street and is not the kind of circus which has three rings and sideshows.

But Flossie shrugged and asked, pointing to the statue, "Who's that boy with the bow and arrows?"

"He's Cupid. His Greek name is Eros, and he was called the god of love."

"Well, I just love him," said Flossie, smiling. "And I love London too."

Freddie, meanwhile, was looking back from where they had come. The little boy looked about at the bright, flashing signs. He seemed confused. "Mr. Bobby," he said, looking up at the officer, "I think we're lost."

"Don't worry, little Yank," the kind man replied. "I'm leaving here now, and I'll take you back. Where are you staying?"

"At the Park Hotel," Freddie told him. The bobby took each twin by one hand and walked with them along Piccadilly. "I don't think you'd better sightsee in London without your parents," he told them as they reached the Park Hotel.

The other Bobbseys were relieved to see them. They had been inquiring of various people about the children, who said they were sorry they had gone off without permission.

The next morning Gail and Gavin arrived shortly after breakfast. Their father had dropped them off on his way to his office.

"Bert," said Gavin excitedly, "we've found a place where miniature armor is sold."

"And it's near by too," Gail said.

Nan and Bert received permission from their parents to go shopping with the Radfords. Mrs. Bobbsey gave Nan twenty-five dollars of the money which had been collected aboard the *Ocean Princess*. "Spend it wisely," she advised.

The children hurried out of the hotel, crossed Piccadilly, and walked through Green Park. "There's Buckingham Palace," Gail said, pointing to the residence of the royal family.

"It's lovely!" Nan declared.

"We'll see it later," Bert said as Nan slowed her pace. "Let's find the miniature shop first."

Gail and Gavin led them up one street and down another. Finally they reached a shop marked, "Miniatures."

"We can't stay too long," Nan said as they entered the shop, "because Mother and Dad are taking us to the Tower of London later on."

The children were delighted with the miniatures in the store—all kinds of tiny figures, dolls, furniture, and jewelry.

"Look here," Gavin said, going up to one of the shelves. "Here are two figures in armor."

"Boy!" Bert said with enthusiasm. "That's just the kind we want for our castle."

The shopkeeper could be heard in a rear room, rattling dishes. "He must be having his breakfast," said Gail.

The only person in the store besides the children was another customer glancing about. He was a man of medium height, with a gaunt face and thin blond hair.

He sidled up to Bert. Putting the back of his hand to his mouth, he whispered, "This is a high-priced shop, sonny. I know where you can buy all kinds of miniatures much cheaper."

Bert looked up, surprised. Nan, beside him, nudged her twin in warning.

"Come with me," the man continued in low tones. "I'll show you a place where you can get a real bargain."

CHAPTER VIII

A BEEFEATER'S WARNING

THE STRANGE man's slyness caused Bert to become suspicious as well as Nan.

"Why are you in this shop, sir, if you can buy miniatures cheaper somewhere else?" the boy asked.

The man raised his eyebrows, which caused his thin face to look even longer. "I'm not here to buy anything," he said. "Just comparing prices for my friend who owns the other shop."

The stranger took a pencil and paper from his pocket and scribbled down a name and address. He passed it to Bert and with a wink added, "You'll find the best buys in London at my friend's place."

Bert said they did not have time to go there immediately. "But perhaps we'll drop by sometime."

At this moment, the shopkeeper came from the room back of the store. The blond-haired stranger quietly left.

The store owner said with a smile, "And what can Mr. Bumper do for you young'uns today?"

Mr. Bumper had a thin fringe of red hair around a bald head, a red, flowing mustache, and a ruddy complexion.

"We have all kinds of miniatures," he went on. "Is there something you want especially?"

Nan told him they were looking for miniature armor to be placed in the throne room of their toy castle.

"I have several pieces here," the man said. "Exact copies of the armor of Henry the Eighth."

Reaching into a cabinet behind him, he pulled out the small pieces and set them on the glass counter. Bert, Nan, Gail, and Gavin pressed close to examine them.

"They're beauties," the English boy said as he picked up the tiny armor gingerly in his fingers.

Mr. Bumper told the children that such tiny miniatures were difficult to make. "It takes a skilled craftsman many days to turn out one," he said.

"How much are they?" Nan asked. "In American dollars, I mean."

The proprietor estimated the cost quickly in

his head. "These two suits of armor cost five dollars apiece."

Bert and Nan looked at each other questioningly. Should they make this purchase now or shop about in order to compare prices?

Nan spoke up. "They're lovely, but we'd like to talk it over with our parents before buying the armor."

"As you wish," Mr. Bumper said politely.

When the children were outside again, Bert said, "That seemed like a high price, Gavin. What do you think?"

"It sounds reasonable to me," their friend replied. "But Nan is right. Perhaps we should shop around."

"How about trying the place that other fellow mentioned?" Bert said, pulling the piece of paper from his pocket.

Gavin looked at the address and said that the shop was located in a shabby section of the city. "It's a jolly long stroll from here."

"Well, anyhow," Bert said, glancing at his wrist watch, "we don't have time to go now. Let's hurry back to the hotel. We don't want to be late for our trip to the Tower of London."

The sky, which had been overcast when the children left the hotel, now had cleared. The sun shone brilliantly on tulip beds which flanked the walks through the park. Reaching the hotel,

Bert and Nan told their mother about the shop and the strange man.

"I'm glad you didn't go to the other place," Mrs. Bobbsey said. "We're having an early lunch."

Mr. Bobbsey had left shortly after breakfast to attend the lumbermen's all-day conference. Mrs. Bobbsey and the six children went into the hotel restaurant. After Bert had seated his mother, the other children took their places at the large round table. The waiter handed each of them a menu, but Freddie did not look at his. Instead, the little boy's eyes roved over the room.

On the far side, in a corner near a large window, was a wooden table. On it stood a large black bird.

"Wowie!" Freddie exclaimed. "What's that?"

"A raven," the waiter replied, smiling. "But the poor chap is stuffed."

Freddie did not know what was meant. Was the raven stuffed from eating too much in the dining room? Or had he died and been stuffed by a taxidermist? He asked the waiter, who laughed.

"The raven is no longer alive. He used to roam the Tower of London and to be exact he lived for forty-four years. We keep him here as a curiosity for tourists to see."

During luncheon, Freddie and Flossie kept

glancing up from their sandwiches to stare at the stuffed raven. Finally Freddie said, "Flossie, we're going to see some real ones this afternoon. Remember?"

"And will we see the very bird that stole the diamond from the lady's ring?" Flossie asked.

"Oh, you've heard about that?" Gavin remarked. "Funny thing that."

"Was the diamond ever found?" Bert asked.

Gavin said that no one knew for certain whether the story was real or make-believe. "At any rate," he added, "no diamond has been reported found anywhere."

After drinking their milk and eating dainty pastries called "banana pretties," the Bobbseys and their friends departed for the Tower of London.

Two small taxis carried them through the narrow streets. Finally they went over London Bridge which crossed the Thames River near the Tower of London.

"There it is," Gail said as they all piled out of the taxis.

The Bobbsey twins looked at the high walls and turrets in awe. "Is that the Tower?" Bert asked. "It's more like a huge fortress!"

The Radfords laughed, as Nan said, "I thought the Tower of London was just one big tower."

"Lots of Americans think that," Gavin said, as they walked down a street toward the entrance gate. "There are many stone buildings, each with at least one tower."

"It's sure a big place!" Freddie remarked as they strolled through a gate and went inside the grounds.

Gavin told the Bobbseys the Tower grounds covered eighteen acres of land. They were guarded by thirteen towers built along the high, square wall that surrounded them.

Along the Thames River were six more towers. Everything was circled by a deep moat of water which was now filled in and was dry and grassy.

"This place," said Gail, "was once a fortress. And it's also been a palace and a prison."

"Also the royal mint," Gavin added. "Lots of money was made here. And it had the royal menagerie too."

"Oh, let's see the animals," Flossie said, remembering her disappointment at Piccadilly Circus. But Gavin told her the Lion Tower, near the spot where they were standing, was no longer used as a zoo.

"The highest and most important building," said Gail, "is the Great Tower, or Keep, called the White Tower. That stands right in the center. Come, I'll show it to you."

The Bobbseys followed the Radford children and gazed at the enormous building with a high turret on each of its four corners.

"Originally, the only entrance to the Keep was on the south side under the Bloody Tower," Gavin said, and Nan shuddered.

"And now," Gail spoke up, "would you like to look at the crown jewels?"

"Oh, yes," the twins said.

They joined a line of visitors who were waiting at Wakefield Tower. Mrs. Bobbsey paid a few coins for them to enter. Then they walked up a stone stairway, entering a room in which stood an immense glass case. What a glitter came from inside it!

"Look at those diamonds and emeralds!" exclaimed Nan. "Everything is beautiful!"

Pressing close to the glass, the Bobbseys and the Radford children walked slowly about the fantastic exhibit. It included kings' and queens' crowns set with precious gems.

"This Imperial State Crown," said Gavin, "was made for the coronation of Queen Victoria in 1838. See the big ruby in it?"

"Why, it's an inch wide!" Nan declared.

Gavin nodded. "The ruby was given to our nobleman, the Black Prince, by Pedro the Cruel after he lost a battle against us."

Other regalia included a pair of gold and enamel bracelets, but Nan continued to stare at the Imperial State Crown. Gail whispered, "It has nearly 3,000 diamonds and 300 other precious stones in it."

"It's simply gorgeous," Nan said.

Bert and Freddie were more interested in the

gold spurs of St. George, the jewel-encrusted swords of state, and the ornate trumpets used in the coronation ceremonies.

"What if someone should try to steal the jewels!" Nan said to Gail.

"Don't worry about that, Nan," came the reply. "There's a good alarm system here. Besides, the Tower is well guarded by the Yeoman Warders."

"The who?"

"The Beefeaters," Nan's friend replied, smiling. "We'll see them in a moment."

After the Bobbseys had viewed the regal splendor of hundreds of years of British royalty, they descended the stone steps once more and went outdoors.

"There's a Beefeater," Gail said, indicating a man standing beside a patch of greensward.

The man's clothes were entirely different from anything the Bobbsey twins had ever seen. He wore a red, belted tunic down to his knees. It was decorated with stripes of black and gold. Around his neck was a white ruff, and on his head rested a flat-brimmed black hat.

"When does he eat all the beef?" Freddie piped up. The Radfords laughed, and Gavin said, "You must learn why they're called Beefeaters."

The boy explained that the guards of the ancient castle who protected the king often had waited on the royal table. "Therefore they were called Buffeteers," Gavin went on. "The word Buffeteers gradually came to be Beefeaters."

"Then it has nothing to do with beef?" Freddie asked, a little disappointed.

"Absolutely nothing," Gavin declared.

"Oh, look!" Nan said suddenly.

Strutting on the grass behind the Beefeater were several ravens. The awkward birds walked along with jerky steps pecking at the ground.

"They're just like the one at the hotel!" Flossie cried out. "Only these aren't stuffed."

She and Freddie approached the birds cautiously. "I'd like to see one real close," Flossie remarked.

The Beefeater, hearing this, smiled. He walked over to the largest of the ravens, picked him up, and perched the bird on his left elbow. "This is Old Blackie," he said. "The one who is supposed to have swallowed the diamond."

"Do you think he did?" Bert asked the yeoman warder.

"I doubt it. I'm jolly well certain it's just a hoax."

"May I take your picture, please, sir?" Nan asked.

"Righto."

Mrs. Bobbsey, who had brought her camera along, handed it to Nan.

With Freddie and Flossie looking on, Nan snapped several pictures of the Beefeater and the raven. All this time Flossie inched closer to the black bird. She put out her hand to pat the glistening black feathers.

"Careful, little girl," the Beefeater said. "Old Blackie can't fly away, but he—"

Blackie acted fast. Darting his beak forward, he pecked at Flossie's finger.

"Ow!" she cried out and leaped back. There was a tiny red mark where the raven's beak had pinched her finger.

The yeoman warder chuckled and told the children that the ravens were not friendly creatures. Then he put Old Blackie down and the bird walked away disdainfully.

While Nan had been taking the pictures Bert had spied a man out of the corner of his eye. The fellow, with a black, well-trimmed beard and natty clothes, was watching the Bobbseys.

After Nan had returned the camera to her mother, Bert whispered, "Nan, look at that fellow over there."

His twin turned her head slowly, then drew in her breath. "Bert," she said, "could he be Silver Smitty?"

"We can't accuse him outright," Bert said, "but he certainly looks a lot like the fellow who ran out of Mr. Warwick's shop."

Nan thought they should tell the Beefeater their suspicions. The yeoman warder had wandered some distance away, and was talking with another group of tourists. Nan and Bert hastened over to the Tower guard. The Beefeater listened intently to their suspicions.

"Where is this man you speak of?" he asked, looking about.

"Right over— He's gone!" Nan said, dismayed.

Just then Freddie ran up and exclaimed, "Blackie's gone. I can't find him anywhere!"

CHAPTER IX

THE TRAFALGAR SQUARE TUSSLE

"YOU say Old Blackie is missing?" the beefeater asked in amazement. He glanced about,
counting the remaining birds. The largest raven
was nowhere to be seen.

"Maybe the suspicious-looking man took
him," Nan remarked.

Immediately, the Beefeater sounded an alarm,
and other guards covered the exit to the Tower
of London. But after a careful look at all the
visitors, the yeoman warders admitted that Old
Blackie's kidnapper had escaped. They asked
the Bobbseys to describe the suspicious-looking
man again.

When Bert finished, one of the warders burst
out, "I say, I saw a man answering that description. He was carrying a black bag."

"Large enough to put Old Blackie in?" Bert
asked.

"Yes, that must have been our man."

The yeoman warders assured the children that the police would keep on searching for the man. The Bobbseys and Radfords promised to be on the lookout too.

The twins and their friends stayed long enough to walk about the grounds of the Tower of London and gaze at the many buildings. Gavin led them into the Horse Armoury. Here stood statues of men fully covered in armor.

"And see this make-believe horse," said Flossie. "He's 'most all covered up, too, like his rider."

Finally the sightseers made their way through a gate. They came out onto the broad plaza facing the Thames River. It was fringed with a battery of old-time cannons.

At once Freddie climbed onto one of the cannons. "I'm a pirate!" he called out. "Boom! Boom!"

Mrs. Bobbsey smiled. "Aren't you and the other pirates getting hungry?" she asked. "I think we'd better go back to the hotel now."

Soon after they returned, Mr. Radford called for his children.

"Thank you so much for showing us around," Nan said.

"Same here," Bert added. "London sure is a swell place."

"Cheerio!" their friends said.

After supper the Bobbsey family gathered in the largest bedroom. Bert telephoned to the London police. He asked whether Old Blackie had been found.

"No, lad. Not yet," was the answer.

Bert turned to the others. "There is something mysterious going on," he said. "And I think it might have to do with the robbery in Lakeport."

"You mean we've carried a mystery right across the Atlantic Ocean?" Flossie asked, wide-eyed.

Mr. Bobbsey smiled and took the little girl on his knee. "You might say it's an international case," he said. "That means world-wide."

"And we'll solve it too," declared Bert with determination.

Next day being Sunday, the Bobbseys went to church in the morning. Their afternoon would be spent sightseeing in Trafalgar Square. They walked from the hotel to Piccadilly Circus, then turned right. Soon afterward they arrived at a vast open place, thronged with people.

From the center of this square rose a tall marble column. Atop it stood a statue of Admiral Nelson.

Mr. Bobbsey said, "This man was responsible for a great sea victory at Trafalgar. He's one of England's great heroes."

At the base of the statue, a gigantic stone lion looked out at the visitors. On Sundays many people came to feed the pigeons.

"How tame they are!" Nan remarked, as several of the friendly birds strayed over to her.

"I say, would you care to feed them?" asked a boy standing near by. He held a brown bag, containing pieces of stale bread.

"Why yes, thank you," Nan answered, smiling.

The boy handed her a slice of bread. She broke it into bits and scattered them at her feet. Immediately a dozen pigeons swooped down to gobble the food.

Freddie had come to his sister's side. The friendly English boy handed a crust to him.

Instantly there was a mischievous look in Freddie's eyes. He said, "I have an idea," and set the piece of bread on top of his head.

Swoop! A pigeon landed on the little fellow's hair, picked up the bread, and flew off.

"Ha, ha! It worked!" Freddie cried gleefully.

Flossie wanted to try the same stunt, so Freddie gave her a crust. The onlookers laughed to see the stunt. Soon many of the small children standing about were doing the same thing.

"What a picture!" Mrs. Bobbsey said, laughing, as the fluttering birds swooped down on the heads of the children. She took several snaps.

Nan looked up at one of the great stone lions. Seated on its head was a bird, too.

"Look, Bert!" she said. "There's a black pigeon, and he seems to be hurt." One of the bird's wings looked as if it were twisted.

Kind-hearted Nan walked closer for a better

look. Suddenly she stopped and called out, "Bert! This isn't a pigeon at all!"

Her brother hurried to her side and gazed at the strange bird.

"Nan, you're right! That's a raven!"

"His wings have been clipped! This must be Old Blackie!" Nan cried out.

The twins' exclamations brought Mr. and Mrs. Bobbsey, the smaller twins, and near-by onlookers to the scene.

"Old Blackie?" one of the Londoners asked. "Isn't he the raven missing from the Tower?"

"Yes, he is," Nan said, "but how can we get hold of him? He may peck us."

"I'll get him," Bert volunteered. "He's probably so scared he'll be glad to have a friend."

"All right, but keep your face away from him," said Mr. Bobbsey.

He boosted his son up onto the large granite block where the lion sat. Shielding his face, Bert reached up toward the raven. But as he did, the bird fluttered. He landed on Mr. Bobbsey's left shoulder.

"Grab him, Dad!" Bert cried out.

As Mr. Bobbsey took the bird in his hands, it made no attempt to peck him.

"Let's take him back to the Tower," Nan said. She stroked the frightened raven. "Don't be afraid. If you're hurt, the Beefeaters will take care of you."

Just then a man standing at the edge of the crowd elbowed his way forward. He had a thin, sallow face and light sandy hair. "Give me my pigeon!" he demanded, roughly making his way toward Mr. Bobbsey.

"Nan!" Bert said, clutching his sister's arm. "Isn't that the fellow we saw at the miniature shop yesterday?"

"Of course! What does he want here?"

The man made his wants known immediately. "That pigeon belongs to me," he said. "Hand it over."

"But it's not a pigeon," Mr. Bobbsey protested. "This is Old Blackie from the Tower of London."

"It belongs to me," the rude fellow protested.

He reached for the raven, but Mr. Bobbsey held the bird away from him. "Give me some proof of ownership, and you may have him."

"I don't have to prove anything," the man growled.

This time he tried to grab the bird. But Mr. Bobbsey held it away from him in his right hand and fended the fellow off with his left. In the struggle the man pushed Mr. Bobbsey, and the twins' father shoved him back. The fellow teetered. Then he fell backward into the arms of a man among the crowd standing about.

"I say, you're a bally nuisance, old fellow.

You'd better get out of here," the man warned, "before I call a bobby."

The troublemaker muttered something under his breath and disappeared into the Trafalgar Square crowd.

"Now are we going to take Old Blackie back to the Tower?" Flossie asked.

"Yes," Mr. Bobbsey answered. "Right away."

"I'll help you," offered a bystander who was an American. "I have my car near by. It's large enough to carry all of you. Come with me."

The drive to the Tower did not take long. Mr. Bobbsey thanked the friendly driver as the family got out. They made their way at once to the yeoman warder with whom they had spoken the afternoon before.

"Mr. Beefeater," Freddie said, running up to the tower guard, "we found Old Blackie."

"By Jove, you have," the man replied, smiling as he took the bird from Mr. Bobbsey's hands.

"We think he's hurt," Nan declared.

The Beefeater examined the bird's wing and agreed that somehow Old Blackie had been injured. "I'll take him to a veterinarian right away," the guard said and thanked the Bobbseys again for finding the raven.

Leaving the Tower, the Bobbsey family strolled once more through the streets of London, looking in shopwindows.

Late in the afternoon they reached their hotel. As Bert went to the desk for the key to their suite, the clerk said, "There's a message for your father."

He reached into the Bobbseys' mailbox and handed the twins' father an envelope.

Mr. Bobbsey opened it, and a frown came over his face.

"Is something wrong, dear?" his wife asked.

"Very wrong," Mr. Bobbsey replied. He took his family aside and quietly read them the note. It began:

"Get the raven back for me or you will be in danger."

"Oh!" Nan gasped.

"This is terrible," Mrs. Bobbsey said.

Her husband read the rest of the note. It gave directions for Old Blackie to be left beside a certain bench in Green Park at nine o'clock that evening.

"Oh, what are we going to do?" wailed Flossie.

Suddenly Bert snapped his fingers. "Dad, I have an idea!" he exclaimed.

CHAPTER X

THE PALACE PARADE

"WE COULD fool the person who sent that note, Dad!" Bert said, his eyes flashing.

"How?" Nan asked.

"Remember the stuffed raven in the hotel dining room?" her twin reminded her. "Perhaps we can borrow it."

Bert's plan was to place the stuffed raven at the spot designated in the note. "Then we can lie in wait and pounce on the fellow when he comes to get it," he said.

"Gracious! You can't do that alone!" Mrs. Bobbsey protested.

"Dad and I could do it," Bert said.

"And me too," Nan pleaded, not wishing to be left out of the adventure.

"Let's talk this over in our rooms," Mrs. Bobbsey suggested, "before we borrow the stuffed raven."

They went upstairs to discuss the mystery. "How did Old Blackie get to the perch on Trafalgar Square?" Nan asked.

"And who was the blond-haired stranger who tried to snatch the raven away? And why is Old Blackie so valuable to the thieves?" Bert added.

Mr. Bobbsey reasoned that such a powerful bird might have wriggled free of his captors and been wounded in the escape. But it did not answer the question of why he was stolen.

Bert looked at his watch. "Dad, don't you think we'd better find out if we may have the stuffed raven?"

"I'll phone the manager now," Mr. Bobbsey promised.

After he explained why the Bobbseys were eager to borrow the stuffed raven, the manager said, "It's a most unusual request, Mr. Bobbsey. But as long as you are in charge, you may borrow the bird. By the way, we call him Cedric."

"Thank you very much," Mr. Bobbsey replied, and hung up.

"Cedric is ours for the evening," he said.

"Who?" the youngsters chorused.

"Cedric, the stuffed raven." Their father chuckled.

Bert and Nan hurried downstairs to get the bird. A few minutes later, they brought Cedric to their parents' room.

Excitement mounted as the hour of nine drew near. At eight-forty, Bert put Cedric in a sack. He and his father and Nan left the hotel and walked across the street into Green Park.

The fifth bench on the right from the park entrance was easy to find. Bert took Cedric out of the sack, placed him in some high grass, and tied one of the bird's legs to the iron arm-rest.

"That will make him look as if he were alive," the boy remarked, grinning.

"Now to locate a good hiding place," Mr. Bobbsey said, glancing around.

"How about over there?" Nan asked, pointing to a screen of low bushes near the bench.

"Perfect," her father agreed.

The three watchers crouched behind the greenery. It was growing dark rapidly. Bert occasionally glanced at his watch. The minutes ticked by so slowly!

"Will that man come?" he thought to himself. "Or are we the ones who are going to be fooled?"

A few minutes before nine, the Bobbseys quit whispering and waited tensely. Out of the semidarkness, they suddenly saw a man touching the bench. A rather large hat was drawn low over his forehead and his coat collar was turned up. The fellow took a few steps, then halted. After glancing around cautiously, he stepped forward again.

Nan nudged her brother. "He sees the bird," she whispered.

Now the lurking figure paused by the bench and glanced up and down the path.

"Get him now, Dad," Bert said in a small voice.

As the fellow was about to bend over, a policeman suddenly appeared out of the gloom. He was walking briskly along. Seeing him, the man straightened up and made off on the double.

"He left the bird!" Bert cried.

"Come on," Mr. Bobbsey said, "we'll try to catch him anyway."

They dashed out of hiding toward the bench. The bobby noticed their haste. "Halt!" he cried.

Mr. Bobbsey, Bert, and Nan stopped. "We were chasing a thief," Mr. Bobbsey said.

"He was just about to take Cedric," Nan added, pointing at the raven still tied to the bench.

"Thief? Cedric? I say, what's all this about?" the bobby demanded.

"We tied the raven to the bench, sir, so we could catch the man who wrote the threatening note," Bert said excitedly.

He and Nan wished to chase the shadowy figure, but by now it was too late. The fellow had made a getaway.

"Now let's start from the beginning," the

policeman said, perplexed by the odd story.

Bert told the bobby everything that had happened, starting with the theft at Mr. Warwick's shop in Lakeport. "So we used Cedric as a decoy to capture the person who wrote the note," Bert concluded.

"I'm sorry I didn't know that," the officer apologized. "Perhaps we could have caught the man. But by now he's a long way from here. What did he look like?"

Nan told what little they knew, and the officer promised to be on the lookout for the man. Bert now picked up Cedric, and the three Bobbseys returned with the bird to the hotel.

"It's a shame your little scheme didn't work, Bert," Nan consoled her twin. "But you may get another chance."

The Bobbseys slept soundly, but Bert was awakened by the ringing of the phone in his room.

"Hello," he said sleepily.

"Cheerio," said Gavin Radford's voice. "I know it's early, fellow. But I have a chance to ride into the city with Papa. If you have no plans, how about our visiting the miniature shop recommended by the blond man? Perhaps we can pick up a clue."

"Come ahead, and listen to this." Bert related what had happened the evening before.

"I say, what a show!" said the English boy. "Now I'm more eager than ever to play detective."

Gavin rapped on the Bobbseys' door shortly before nine o'clock. "Good morning, Mr. and Mrs. Bobbsey," he said, stepping inside. Then he added, "Ready, Bert?"

Mrs. Bobbsey asked the boys to be sure to return by ten-thirty. "We're going over to Buckingham Palace to watch the changing of the guard," she said.

"You'll like that," Gavin remarked.

Bert put the new magnifying glass in his pocket in order to examine any miniatures he might see. Then he and Gavin hurried toward the elevator.

Walking briskly along the crowded streets, the boys finally located the store. It was a dingy basement shop at the foot of steep stone steps. The boys descended them. As Bert opened the door, a tinkling bell on it sounded.

The shop was small with a door leading to a back room. Nobody was in sight. The two chums glanced about. The miniatures on display looked rusted and tarnished.

"No wonder they sell things cheaper," Bert said in a low voice, walking to the rear. "I wonder where—"

He stopped speaking suddenly as he looked

through the door to the rear room. On a shelf directly in the line of sight was something that made the boy start. It was a miniature television set!

"Gavin," Bert whispered, pointing, "I think it's the same one that was stolen in Lakeport!"

"Are you certain?" Gavin asked.

"I'm so sure that I'm going to call Dad," the Bobbsey boy said, turning to the door. "Come on, Gavin."

Gavin followed him up the steps. Bert hailed a taxicab and in a few minutes they reached the hotel.

"Wait for me, please," Bert asked the cabbie.

Bert met his father walking through the lobby. "Dad!" the boy called, "come with me quick! I need your help!"

Mr. Bobbsey followed his son through the revolving door and out into the street again. They hopped into the cab.

"Take us back where we came from, please," Bert told the driver.

As they started off, Mr. Bobbsey said "What's this all about?"

After Bert had told him, his father urged the cabbie to hurry.

When they arrived at the shop, the shelf where the miniature television had stood was empty!

Just then a short, stout man, stooped, and

wearing thick, horn-rimmed glasses, came from the back room. Bert decided he was very near-sighted, because he held his face close to the boy's to see him.

"You want something?" the man asked.

At first Bert was at a loss for words. "Yes—er—why, I wanted to look at that miniature TV you had here a few minutes ago."

The shopkeeper blinked and drew back. "Miniature television, you say? I've never had one of 'em," he said.

Mr. Bobbsey spoke up. "My son said he saw one here a short time ago."

"Your son could jolly well be mistaken," the man said stiffly.

"I think not," Gavin declared. "I saw it my-self."

The shopkeeper bristled. "I won't have a couple of upstarts doubting me word!"

Mr. Bobbsey said quietly, "I guess there's nothing more we can do about it just now."

He started out the door, and the two boys fol-lowed up the steps. They were nearly bumped into by a man who came rushing down.

He was carrying the miniature television!

Bert stood electrified as the man brushed past him and opened the shop door.

"This set is imperfect," the customer boomed. "One of the dials is missing."

Hearing this, Bert, Gavin, and Mr. Bobbsey raced back into the shop. The proprietor glanced nervously about from one to the other. "You didn't buy that television here, sir," he protested.

"What!" the customer cried out. "You dare say that to me, Roscoe Albemarle! Why, you—"

"Let me see the set, if you will, sir," Bert said, stepping up with his magnifying glass.

The man handed over the set, and Bert turned it upside down. Then with the magnifying glass he searched for the telltale initials, M and W, shaped like two diamonds side by side.

"Dad! Here it is!" He turned to Mr. Albemarle.

"Sir," he said, "this is a stolen set." Bert produced the missing knob, which the ship's detective had returned to him. He pressed it into place in the miniature TV.

"I might have guessed the truth, Mr. Albemarle," the customer said. "The price was ridiculously low." With that he reached over the counter and grasped the proprietor by the lapels of his coat.

"Hurry! Call a bobby!" he ordered.

Gavin dashed into the street and returned in a few minutes with an officer. After accusations by Bert Bobbsey, which the disgruntled Mr. Albemarle denied, the policeman said to Bert, "Thank you very much for your assistance." He took the TV set as evidence. Then, beckoning to the shopkeeper, he said, "Come with me."

As Mr. Bobbsey and the two boys climbed the steps to the street, Bert said, "We'd better hurry,

Dad, or we won't be in time for the changing of the guard."

Back at the hotel, meanwhile, Mrs. Bobbsey waited for her husband and Bert to return. "Oh dear," she said, glancing at her watch. "It's nearly time for us to be at Buckingham Palace. I wonder what's delaying your father and Bert and Gavin?"

Nan suggested that they walk across the park to Buckingham Palace. "I'm sure Dad will meet us there," she said.

Her mother agreed to do this. Taking Freddie and Flossie by the hand, she crossed the street and hastened through Green Park. Already scores of people had gathered before the high iron fence surrounding the royal residence. The Union Jack was flying over the palace, indicating that the royal family was at home. The colorful sentries standing before their boxes delighted Freddie and Flossie.

Freddie giggled. "They look like great big toy wooden soldiers, Mother."

"What are they wearing on their heads?" Flossie asked, looking up at the tall, fur "busbies," firmly held in place on the heads of the sentries with chin straps.

Freddie and Flossie edged up to one of the men and gazed into his face. The young soldier did not change his expression. Not a muscle in his face moved.

"Do you think he's mad at us?" Freddie asked his sister.

"We didn't do anything," the little girl said.

"I'll bet I can make him laugh," said Freddie, putting two fingers to the sides of his mouth. He stretched his face into a ludicrous position.

"Don't do that, Freddie," Flossie whispered.

The sentry looked down at the two children, but his expression did not change. Then Freddie made some funny noises.

"It's no use," Flossie declared. Then she said, "Look! They're changing the guard now!"

The children peered through the iron fence. They saw the group of red-coated soldiers leave their posts, form a neat line, and march briskly out of the courtyard. At almost the same instant, another group of sentries appeared to take over the guard. At this moment a band began to play stirring martial music.

"Hurray! Hurray! Here comes a parade!" Freddie shouted.

Along with Nan and their mother, Freddie and Flossie hastened to the curb to watch the guards parade past.

Freddie's heart beat faster at the sound of the heroic music. "I want to parade with them!" he told his twin.

"But you can't, Freddie!" Flossie said.

Freddie would not be stopped. He dashed into the street and tried to get in step beside a tall, red-coated soldier.

"Come back, Freddie!" Mrs. Bobbsey called.

CHAPTER XI

THE LITTLE REDCOAT

GIGGLING, but a little worried, Flossie watched her twin. Freddie was trying to match strides with one of the tall, red-coated guards marching in front of Buckingham Palace.

But the little boy's legs were far too short. Freddie had to trot to keep up with the parade, as the band stepped along at a lively gait before the cheering onlookers.

"Freddie, you imp!" Mrs. Bobbsey called to him. "Come back here!" The horns were playing so loudly, however, that Freddie could not hear her.

It was at this moment that Mr. Bobbsey, Bert, and Gavin arrived at the scene.

"Look!" Bert cried out. "Isn't that Freddie marching along there?"

"It certainly is," his father replied.

114

Without a word Gavin ran into the street, took Freddie by the hand, and led him back to the curb. The spectators clapped and laughed.

After the parade had passed the palace, Bert told the others what had happened at the miniature shop.

"Are you sure it was the same tiny television set?" Nan asked.

Bert told her about the missing knob, and also the trademark, M.W.

"Yes," Gavin said. "We caught the old monster red-handed."

Mr. Bobbsey said he thought the fellow's arrest might lead to the capture of Silver Smitty. "That is, if the shopkeeper confesses and tells the police how he came to have Mr. Warwick's stolen property."

Flossie, meanwhile, was gazing through the iron bars of the fence at the palace windows. Suddenly she exclaimed, "Oh, look! I see the Princess!"

"Where?" Nan asked, wheeling about.

"Up there. She's waving a handkerchief."

All the children turned their eyes to the window where Flossie pointed.

"How do you know it's the Princess?" said Bert doubtfully.

" 'Cause she's waving at us children," Flossie replied earnestly.

The window was too far away for the Bobbseys to see the figure clearly. But Gavin said
that sometimes members of the royal family did
wave at the crowds gathered below to watch the
changing of the guard.

"And now," said Mrs. Bobbsey, "Nan and
Flossie and Freddie and I have a surprise to tell
you boys. Mrs. Radford phoned to invite all of
us out to their house this afternoon."

"Swell!" Bert grinned.

His mother said that Mr. Radford had arranged his work so he would be able to call for
Gavin and the Bobbseys after luncheon.

"Dad and I shan't be able to go," she went
on. "We must attend a special party the president
of the lumbermen's association is giving."

Gavin was beaming. "I say, Mama always
does the most interesting things. We'll have a
lot of fun."

The English boy remained with the Bobbsey
twins for luncheon. Not long afterward, his father called at the hotel. "I think we can all fit
into my car," he said. To Mrs. Bobbsey he
added, "I will see that your twins get home
safely after teatime."

Freddie and Flossie skipped through the
lobby with Bert, Nan, and Gavin following.
When they reached the curb, Gavin slid into
the seat beside his father. Bert and Nan held

Freddie and Flossie on their laps in the back seat.

After driving along many city streets, Mr. Radford reached the outskirts. The car rolled through the countryside, past sweet-smelling meadows, rimmed with spring flowers. Then he turned into a side road, and presently they stopped before a quaint-looking house with a thatched roof.

"Here we are," Gavin said, getting out.

"What a darling place!" Nan exclaimed.

"It's bee-yoo-ti-ful!" Flossie declared.

The Radford home was set a good distance away from neighboring houses on either side. Nan said it reminded her of a picture-book cottage in her geography book.

Two beds of delphinium and roses bloomed in front of the house. There were other artistic flowerbeds here and there. The rear of the property was bounded by a tall hawthorne hedge which boxed in an emerald-green lawn.

Mrs. Radford and Gail hurried out of the house to greet their guests. After showing them about the place, Mrs. Radford told Nan that Gail and Gavin had some miniature toys they had received for Christmas several years before.

"They're stored in the attic right now. Would you like to see them?"

"Oh, yes!" the Bobbseys chorused.

As the English children led them through the house, the Americans noticed that each room had a fireplace. When Bert remarked about this, Gavin said, "That's to keep us warm on chilly, damp days. We don't have a lot of heat in our homes, you know."

A small stairway led from the second floor to a large attic. It was filled with trunks, old bits of bric-a-brac, and toys which Gail and Gavin had outgrown. Freddie found a tricycle which was too small even for him, while Bert examined an electric train set.

"Here's where the miniatures are," Gail said, pulling out a brown carton from under the eaves. When she opened it, Nan exclaimed, "Oh, a tiny canopy bed! And look at the little dresser!"

"Here are the chairs," Gail said, as she held the Lilliputian pieces in the palm of her hand.

As Nan admired the tiny set, Gail went on, "Would you like to take these back to America for the hospital children?"

"Oh, I wouldn't want to take away your toys. Thank you just the same."

"But you must take them," Gail insisted. "I don't play with them any more."

Touched by her English friend's generosity, Nan accepted the antique miniature bedroom set for the toy castle. She thanked Gail with a hug.

Bert, Gavin, and Freddie, tiring of the attic exploration before the girls did, went downstairs to the yard to play ball. Half an hour later, Gail, Flossie, and Nan appeared. Nan carried a mysterious brown bag under one arm, and all the girls were giggling.

"What's the joke?" Bert asked.

"You'll see," Nan teased him.

"Please tell me, Ducks," Gavin begged his sister.

But the boys had to contain their curiosity while the girls ran behind a rose arbor. "Don't look until we tell you," Gail begged them.

Bert shrugged as the boys turned their backs. "This had better be funny," he said.

After they had waited a few moments, Nan cried out, "All right, now you can look!" With that she and Gail sang out, "Boom-da-de-da-da! Boom-da-de-da-da!"

The boys wheeled about to see Flossie Bobbsey parading toward them. She wore an old red coat several sizes too large for her. On the little girl's head was a black fur muff, which looked like a busby. To complete her outfit, Flossie carried a short broom handle over her shoulder.

"I'm a redcoat!" she exclaimed gleefully.

"Hurray for the palace guard!" Gail said.

"Not bad," Bert said. All the boys were grinning.

"Let me try it on, Flossie," her twin begged, running up to her.

"All right," Flossie agreed. She took off the red coat which Gail had found in the attic.

Freddie put the coat on. Then he set the busby muff on his head, tilting it.

Freddie stood proud and erect with the broom-stick rifle over his shoulder. He marched about the yard, whistling a military tune. But he had to hold his head high in order to see where he was going. As he strolled along, the muff fell lower.

"Watch where you're going!" Bert cried out.

Freddie walked straight into a rosebush!
"Ouch!" he yelled and jumped back. The
busby fell to the grass.

Freddie bent down, picked up his headgear,
and set off in the opposite direction. The others
giggled.

While Freddie and Flossie took turns playing
palace guard, Bert and Gavin had fun playing
toss with a red rubber ball. In the meantime
Gail and Nan had walked into the garage, where
two bicycles stood side by side.

"Let's take a ride and visit my Aunt Jennifer,"
Gail proposed. She explained that her aunt
lived about a quarter of a mile away.

"You'll love her," Gail went on. "Aunt Jennifer is very interesting."

Gail told her mother where she and Nan
were going. Then the girls mounted the bicycles
and started pedaling down the street. For a while
they rode side by side, until a car approached
them. The driver honked his horn.

Nan, forgetting that she was on an English
road, swerved to the right side of the road instead of to the left.

"Nan!" her friend cried excitedly. "Over this
way. Quickly!"

Nan turned her handlebars to the left and
pedaled hard as the oncoming car whizzed toward her!

CHAPTER XII

ROYAL TWINS

THERE was a squealing of brakes as the driver of the car slowed his vehicle. Nan swerved out of the way just in time.

"I'm so sorry," she said, passing the motorist. The driver, a young man in a tweed suit, grinned. "Careful, little girl. This is not America, you know."

Nan determined to be extra cautious after this when riding on English roads. Keeping far to the left, she and Gail pedaled along the tree-shaded streets of the suburban town. Presently they came to a cottage, smaller than the Radfords', but equally as quaint. It was surrounded by flowers.

"See the pink and white and lavender larkspur?" Gail said, as Nan gazed in admiration at the blooms. "Aunt Jennifer specializes in them."

The girls found Aunt Jennifer, wearing a smock and big straw sun hat, at the rear of the cottage. She was transplanting some seedlings.

"Cheerio, Aunty," said Gail, kissing her aunt. "This is my American friend, Nan Bobbsey."

Nan shook hands with Aunt Jennifer. She was a tall woman with a firm chin and ready smile. She looked much like Gail's father.

"Shall we go inside for a spot of tea?" she suggested.

"Let's have it in the arbor," Gail spoke up. "I love to smell your flowers."

Her aunt called indoors to a maid who presently served little cakes, tea, and milk in a rustic summerhouse at the rear of the garden. There was a small pool in front of it, and Nan was fascinated by the fantailed goldfish swimming about in the water among some pond lilies.

"Tell me all about your family, Nan," Aunt Jennifer said. "And are you enjoying your visit to our country?"

"Oh, yes. I love it."

As Nan sipped her milk, she told about the Bobbsey family and their reason for coming to England. She concluded with the story of the miniature castle and how the twins were looking for suitable furniture in England. "We need some things for the throne room. Do you know where we can find any?"

Gail's aunt set her cup of tea on the table and thought for a moment. Then she said, "If you're going to visit Windsor Castle, I can tell you of a lovely shop near by."

"Mother and Daddy plan to take us there tomorrow," Nan replied.

"Well," Aunt Jennifer said, "very near the entrance of the castle is a small restaurant. Across the street from it is Mrs. Smollen's shop. She makes furniture imitating the pieces to be found in the Queen's Dolls' House. She also sells antique miniatures. I'm sure Mrs. Smollen will have a set of throne-room furniture."

Nan's eyes sparkled in anticipation. "Thank you very much," she said.

Before the girls left her, Aunt Jennifer picked a large bouquet of larkspur for the Bobbseys to enjoy in their hotel rooms. By the time Nan and Gail got back to the Radfords', Gail's mother was ready to drive the twins into London. When they reached the hotel, the children told her what a lovely visit they had had and that they hoped to see them all again soon.

Nan told her parents about Mrs. Smollen's shop. Then Mr. Bobbsey said he had some news too. The police had phoned him, saying the shop proprietor who had been arrested would tell the police nothing about the stolen TV set.

"So the police think he is in league with the

thieves," Mr. Bobbsey went on. "They'll keep him in jail for receiving stolen goods."

"We have more news," Mrs. Bobbsey spoke up. "Your father has rented a car for our trip to Windsor Castle. And it's large enough so nobody will have to sit on anyone else's lap."

"Goody," said Flossie.

They started out next morning. For many miles the road paralleled the Thames River, which flowed gently through vast open fields.

"Here's Runnymede," Mr. Bobbsey said, glancing at a road sign.

"I know what that is!" Bert volunteered. "The place where the Magna Charta was signed centuries ago, giving the English working people more rights."

Soon the outline of Windsor Castle rose against the bright morning sky, its towers and turrets reflecting the rays of the sun.

"How big and majestic!" Nan said.

As Mr. Bobbsey drove the car toward the entrance, Nan noticed Mrs. Smollen's shop. After their father had found a parking place, the children got out and walked toward the gate.

Freddie saluted a sentry smartly. "How is the Queen today?" the little boy asked. Then without waiting for an answer, he took Flossie's hand and ran through the great archway into the castle's vast courtyard.

Mr. and Mrs. Bobbsey stopped long enough to purchase sightseers' tickets. Then they hurried after their excited children. Once inside the gate, the family's attention first was drawn to a tall, round tower situated on a hill. The guidebook which Mrs. Bobbsey had bought told how it had been built by King Henry II in 1180.

"We don't have any buildings as old as this in the United States, do we?" Bert said, as they strolled uphill past the gray tower.

"That's because ours is a young country," Mrs. Bobbsey answered.

The sightseers continued on. After descending a cobblestoned roadway, they stepped inside a magnificent gray stone building, where the royal apartments were and where the Queen's Dolls' House was on display.

What breath-taking sights met their eyes as they walked from room to room of the ancient castle! Great pieces of armor, beautiful paintings, exquisite dinnerware, rooms with statuary and giant crystal chandeliers caused the visitors to stare open-mouthed at the wonders of England's past.

"This is the way one king and queen after another lived for hundreds of years," Nan whispered to the younger twins.

Nan and Flossie were especially thrilled when they saw the Queen's Dolls' House. The front wall had been raised, showing the rooms inside.

"The details are amazing," Mrs. Bobbsey said, as she bent close to the fabulous exhibit.

Nan was especially interested in the tiny sitting room, with its little white chairs. Flossie admired the Queen's bedroom with its high, canopied bed and tiny clock on the wall, surrounded by a golden sunburst.

The dining room, its walls covered with miniature paintings, looked so real that Bert expected wee people to walk in and take their places.

"And look at the garages!" Freddie declared, pointing to the base of the Dolls' House. Five tiny automobiles stood in line, each a perfect copy of real English cars. Freddie would have loved to touch them, but visitors were not allowed to do this.

Mr. Bobbsey was as fascinated as the twins, who lingered for a long while. As they started away from the Queen's Dolls' House, Mr. Bobbsey suddenly was jostled by a heavy-set man.

"So sorry," the man said and hurried off with another group of sightseers.

The twins' father shrugged, and said, "I wonder why he bumped into me. There was plenty of room to get past."

After the Bobbseys had walked through other rooms of the castle which were open to visitors, they started for the exit. Freddie and Flossie fell behind. By the time the others had come to the great doorway, they could not see the small twins.

Mrs. Bobbsey turned about. "Where could they be?"

"Maybe they stayed to look around in one of the rooms," Nan suggested, starting back.

But the young twins were not in sight. "How could they vanish?" Nan asked her mother, as the other Bobbseys descended a flight of stairs. It was flanked by statues of armored knights on horseback.

Several guides were questioned, but said they had not seen the blond-haired twins.

Bert, who had gone on ahead, came back and beckoned to his parents and Nan to follow him. He was grinning.

In the center of a large room stood an immense table. Freddie and Flossie sat on two chairs at the head of the table, their backs to the searchers.

"Listen!" Bert whispered.

"Queen Flossie," Freddie was saying, "is there something you would like your royal maid to do?"

"I want a new embroidered dress, King Freddie."

"You shall have it." The boy clapped his hands, as if summoning his courtiers.

"Make Queen Flossie a new dress, and while you're at it, build a new castle for Mother and Daddy."

"Isn't this fun?" Flossie said, giggling.

Mr. and Mrs. Bobbsey were so amused that they could not scold the little runaways. "All right, Your Royal Highnesses," their father called out. "Let's go!"

The children turned about, startled. The game of King and Queen was over. Obediently, they followed their parents and left Windsor Castle.

"That was a long walk," Mrs. Bobbsey said. She suggested they have a snack at the restaurant and walked in. When they finished a lunch of open roast beef sandwiches and custard, Bert said he wanted to pay for it. He had a pocketful of shillings!

"Go ahead!" Mr. Bobbsey laughed.

As they left the restaurant, Nan asked if they might visit Mrs. Smollen's shop.

"All right, dear," Mrs. Bobbsey said.

When they entered the shop, it seemed to be unattended. The Bobbseys waited for Mrs. Smollen, in the meantime looking at the beautiful silver miniatures.

"Goodness, I wonder where she is," the twins' mother said, after they had browsed about for ten minutes.

Suddenly Bert asked, "What's that noise?"

Everyone stood still. From a small room at the rear came a muffled cry. Mr. Bobbsey hurried to investigate, followed by Bert and Nan.

The room was filled with antique chairs and tables, and at first they saw no one. Then the Bobbseys gasped. Tied to a heavy carved chair was a woman, a gag across her mouth. Mr. Bobbsey freed her instantly.

"I—I've been robbed!" the woman cried. "Call the police!"

Mr. Bobbsey inquired, "Are you Mrs. Smollen?"

"Yes."

"I'll find a policeman," Bert offered, and ran out, while his parents tried to calm the excited shopkeeper.

The boy returned in a few moments with an officer. Mrs. Smollen told him she had been seized by two men and tied to the chair. "They were looking for something in my shop," she said.

"What did they want?" the policeman asked.

"My miniature throne room set," she replied. "It's in the safe. I wouldn't tell them the combination."

Mrs. Smollen declared that the thieves, who wore masks, had snatched several of the miniatures. They had raced out the rear door when they heard the Bobbseys entering the shop.

After making sure Mrs. Smollen was not injured, the policeman hurried off to look for the thieves.

Mrs. Bobbsey told the proprietress that they too were looking for a throne room set. "We won't bother you now," the twins' mother said kindly. "Perhaps we'll come back another time."

"Oh, no," Mrs. Smollen said. "I'm all right, really I am. I'll be happy to show the set to you."

Bert and Nan could hardly wait until she opened her safe. In a few moments she drew out the most exquisite set of miniatures that the children had ever seen.

"They're perfectly lovely!" Nan raved, as the

shopkeeper set the tiny pieces on a square of black velvet.

The miniatures included a king's and queen's throne, inlaid with imitation jewels. There were also two tiny crowns, a sceptre, and four high-backed chairs for the royal attendants. How real the chairs looked with their deep-red tapestry seats!

"This set would make our castle complete!" Bert declared.

Mrs. Smollen smiled at the boy's enthusiasm. "It's expensive," she warned him. The price she quoted, however, was within the amount collected by the Radfords aboard the *Ocean Princess*.

After a whispered conference with her mother, Nan said happily, "We'll buy it, Mrs. Smollen."

"I am so thankful those rascals didn't get the miniatures from me," the woman declared, "and I hope the police catch them soon."

She went to the rear of the store for a cardboard box in which to pack the throne set, but it was not large enough to hold everything. One of the tapestry chairs would not fit in. Mrs. Bobbsey suggested that the chair be wrapped in tissue. "We can slip it into our camera case," she said.

When this was done, Mr. Bobbsey reached into a back pocket for his wallet. A startled look came over his face.

"My wallet—it's gone!" he exclaimed.

CHAPTER XIII

A RIVER CHASE

Mr. Bobbsey looked in one pocket, then another. Still he could not find his wallet. Without money, the twins could not buy the throne room furniture and take it back to America. And furthermore, all the cash the people on the ship had collected had been in the wallet!

"Dad!" Bert exclaimed. "Perhaps that fellow who jostled you at Windsor Castle took your wallet!"

Mr. Bobbsey thought this was possible. He told Bert and Nan to come with him, asking the others to remain at the shop until they returned. The three hurried out of the store, across the street, and approached the castle gate.

As Nan passed through the archway, a thought suddenly occurred to her. "Isn't this where you bought the tickets?"

"Yes, Nan."

"Did you take money from your wallet?"

133

"That's right, I did," Mr. Bobbsey said.

"Then maybe you dropped it here," Nan suggested.

"I'll ask a guard," Bert offered, and hurried up to one of the officers.

Much to the delight of the twins and their father, the officer said yes, a wallet had been found.

"Can you identify it, sir?" he asked, leading the visitors to a small office at one side of the arch.

As soon as Mr. Bobbsey had proved his identity, the wallet was returned to him. "This embarrasses me," he said, flushing a little. "I must be very careful in the future, especially when I'm carrying money that doesn't belong to me."

He returned with Bert and Nan to Mrs. Smollen's Antique Shop and paid for the miniature throne room furniture. By this time, the Englishwoman had regained her composure. Bert and Nan asked more questions about the thieves.

"You say they wore masks?" Bert said. "Did you see what any part of their faces looked like?"

Mrs. Smollen searched her memory for a moment. "I remember now. One of the men had a black beard. I noticed it under the edge of his mask."

"Then it could be Silver Smitty!" Bert said and explained to her who he was. "If we could only get our hands on that thief!"

Bert began to reason that Silver Smitty, since he was so clever, might have made his escape in an unusual way.

"How?" Nan asked.

"Well, maybe by way of the Thames River!"

Mrs. Bobbsey thought this would be a slow way to go if they were trying to avoid the police.

"Bert may be right at that, Mother," Nan defended her twin. She pointed out that a leisurely trip down the Thames toward London might not arouse any suspicion.

"No doubt the police have the same idea, son," Mr. Bobbsey said. "But it wouldn't hurt to inquire."

"I'll ring them up," Mrs. Smollen offered. But she could get no information on the phone.

Bert now asked if he might do a little investigating on his own. "I'll ask some questions along the riverfront. Please wait here for me."

Mr. and Mrs. Bobbsey consented, and Bert hurried off. Soon he was on the bank of the beautiful river which flowed lazily along. Several small boats plied back and forth. Suddenly Bert noticed for the first time the dress of a group of boys on the opposite shore. They wore dark trousers, cutaway jackets, and high, stiff collars. Bert wondered why. The only person close enough for him to ask was a lad paddling by in a two-place kayak.

"Hi!" said Bert, hailing the boy, who was about his own age. "Are those fellows going to a wedding?"

The paddler smiled, and with a strong stroke, came over to where Bert was standing. "I say, you're a stranger here, aren't you?"

"Yes," Bert said. "I'm Bert Bobbsey from the States."

"I'm George Neeley from Birmingham. I'm a student at Eton over there. Those chaps you see are wearing Eton uniforms."

Bert had heard of the famous school for boys, but had not realized it was so close to Windsor Castle.

"George," Bert said, "I'm looking for a clue to a robbery which just took place here."

"Really? Can I be of some help?"

Bert quickly related what had happened and added, "Have you seen a man with a black beard on the river?"

"By Jove, I have," George said. "And what's more, it was a phony beard." He told Bert two men had stepped into a boat on the riverbank not long before. They had started for London at a slow pace. "They didn't see me paddling near by. I noticed one of the fellows pull a false beard from his face."

"What kind of a boat was it?" Bert asked, excited by the discovery he had made.

From George's description of the motorboat, Bert felt it might be the same one that had picked up Silver Smitty from the *Ocean Princess*. Only the color was different.

"It was dark red," George said, and Bert immediately figured the craft had been repainted.

Bert quickly told George that the thief might be riding leisurely along the river to escape notice.

"Then hop in, old boy, and we'll get them!" George offered.

Without hesitation, Bert stepped down into the seat at the front of the kayak. He picked up a paddle at his feet, and together the boys skimmed along the river. They made fast time as they passed several rowboats and a canoe.

"Those men may be faster than I expected," Bert said, as the boys approached a curve in the river.

Rounding it, George suddenly exclaimed, "I say, I see them!"

"Where?"

"Along the river on the right, Bert. See that red boat? Two fellows are tinkering with the motor."

The men were too far away to be recognizable, but Bert had an idea. "Let's drift close to them and take a good look, George."

Acting casual to avoid suspicion, the boys

dipped their paddles slowly into the water. Very gradually they came closer and closer to the motorboat.

"They have engine trouble," Bert said in a low voice. "We're in luck."

The hood of the motor had been raised. Both men, with wrenches in their hands, were working over it.

Suddenly one of the fellows stood erect and scowled. "A fine time for your boat to conk out," he said testily.

"Don't complain," the other man said, looking up at him. "You wanted to go slowly, didn't you? Well, we are—real slow. We're driftin'."

Bert's pulse quickened as he stole a glance at the disgruntled man. The fellow's voice revealed that he was an American. From his slight figure, Bert felt positive that he was the shadowy figure he had seen in the lifeboat aboard the *Ocean Princess*. Silver Smitty!

Bert turned quietly toward George. "Hurry! Let's go back," he whispered.

Once out of earshot of the disabled motorboat, Bert explained excitedly, "George, they're the ones, I'm sure. We'd better get the police!"

The paddle blades dug swiftly and deeply into the placid river, making the kayak zip along. As the two boys reached their starting place, Bert saw his family standing on the shore. He waved

The boys dipped their paddles slowly into the water

to them and called out the news of his discovery.

"We'll have to hurry if we want to catch them," he said as the kayak came to a stop on the riverbank.

Bert quickly introduced his family to George and tried to step out of the kayak at the same time. But in his haste, he missed his footing.

"Be careful, Bert!" George cried. "You'll—"

But Bert had already flipped wildly. Taking a backward somersault, he landed head first in the river!

CHAPTER XIV

AN ANGRY SWAN

ALTHOUGH Bert had taken a rather deep dive, he surfaced quickly. Soaking wet, he pulled himself ashore, grinning in embarrassment.

Mr. Bobbsey and Nan, meanwhile, had hurried off to notify a policeman about the two suspects in the motorboat. "Oh, I hope they catch those bad men," said Flossie, jumping up and down.

Bert shook the water from his sopping wet clothes and apologized for being so clumsy.

"It was my fault," George said. "Sorry. I should have held the kayak closer to the shore." The Eton boy excused himself, saying he would return shortly with some dry clothes for Bert.

"But not that dress uniform," said Bert, grinning. "My American friends wouldn't know me."

141

George chuckled. He paddled rapidly to the other shore and hopped out of his craft. He ran toward the brick building which was his dormitory. The boy returned shortly with a pair of shorts, skivy shirt, socks, and sneakers.

"Here, Bert, I'm sure these will fit you," he said, handing over the clothing.

Bert thanked his friend, who said he must leave now. "Cheerio! And I hope the police catch your man."

The Bobbseys waved good-by, then Mrs. Bobbsey suggested that Bert change his clothes in Mrs. Smollen's back room.

By the time he was dressed, Mr. Bobbsey and Nan arrived. They reported that the police were on their way to seize the suspects on the river. The Bobbseys did not expect to hear anything very soon. They were astounded, therefore, to see two policemen hurrying to the shop. Between them was a sullen-looking prisoner.

"That's one of the men!" Bert cried out, then asked, "Where's the other man?"

"He escaped," a policeman answered.

Both the Bobbseys and the policemen quizzed the prisoner. They learned that he was a petty thief who was wanted in Southampton.

"Was your pal named Silver Smitty?" Bert asked the glowering suspect.

"No. I don't know a bloomin' soul named Silver Smitty. This bloke hired me to give 'im a ride. That's all I know."

Neither the Bobbseys nor the police believed this. "We'll find the other chap," one of the officers said. "He must have escaped in a stolen boat or he's now traveling overland toward London."

The officers wanted to know where the Bobbseys were staying at Windsor. "In case we should capture the other man, we might want you to identify him."

"We weren't planning to stay here," Mrs. Bobbsey spoke up, "but I'm sure we could arrange to if it would help you."

Mr. Bobbsey had to return to London for a meeting that evening and early next day. But he secured accommodations for his family at a quaint inn not far from Windsor Castle. Before starting off, he made arrangements for the twins and their mother to ride down the Thames to Hampton Court next day. He would meet them there with the car.

Flossie clapped her hands in delight when she heard this. "Then we can see the beautiful swans on the river!" she cried.

The hotel clerk, overhearing this, said there were many of the stately white birds swimming gracefully on the river. "In fact," he said, "there are swans the entire length of the Thames. Most of them belong to the Queen."

"Oh," Flossie sighed. "I wish I were a queen!"

After Mr. Bobbsey had driven out of sight, the twins and their mother made themselves comfortable at the inn. All of them hoped to hear from the police, but no word came.

After breakfast next morning, the Bobbseys were paged at the inn. Bert went to the desk where he was met by a rough-looking man wearing a taxi driver's cap.

"Do you want to see the Bobbseys?" Bert asked.

The man said he had been ordered by Mr. Bobbsey to take the family on a sightseeing trip.

"Another one of Dad's surprises," Bert said, and went to tell the others.

The family followed the driver out to the curb, where his cab waited. He held the door open. "Step in," the man said.

Just then Bert noticed another car parked behind the cab. A man was hunched low over the wheel. It looked as if he were trying to hide his face behind a newspaper he was reading.

"Wait a minute, Mother," Bert said. He walked to the car behind in order to get a better look at the fellow. Startled, Bert cried out, "It's Silver Smitty!"

The man behind the wheel did not wait for a further investigation. Starting the motor, he raced away as the Bobbseys looked on, openmouthed with surprise.

Just as quickly, the cabbie leaped into his

empty taxi and with a roar took off behind the fleeing automobile.

"No wonder the police couldn't find Silver Smitty between here and London," Bert exclaimed. "The fellow's still in town."

The boy raced back inside the inn. He asked the desk clerk to phone the police and tell them about the thief and the other man. The call was put in.

Bert returned to his family, who were still outside.

"If that was Silver Smitty," said Nan, "he certainly wants us to leave here. He was actually going to take us away!"

"But why?" Flossie asked.

Freddie suggested that maybe the bad man still thought the Bobbseys had Old Blackie. His mother smiled and showed Freddie a morning newspaper. On the first page was a story reporting that Old Blackie had been returned to the Tower of London.

Nan read the whole story to the younger twins. It said, "Old Blackie feels better, judging by the way he pecked a lady's ankle yesterday afternoon!"

While Mrs. Bobbsey packed their belongings, Bert returned the clothes to George, thanked the Eton boy, and said good-by.

The Bobbseys now went to the river and found the motorboat which would carry them from

Windsor to Hampton Court. The middle-aged pilot, who said his name was Tom, spoke with a Cockney accent. He wore a riverman's cap at a rakish angle.

Tom helped the twins and their mother aboard the comfortable craft. It was a twenty-footer, with a cabin forward and a spacious open deck aft. There were folding chairs for everyone.

" 'Elp yourselves to seats," he said. "I sye, 'tis blarsted warm to-dye."

The Bobbseys smiled as they agreed. The boat left the dock and started down the Thames River toward Hampton Court. Tom told his passengers that this was also an ancient palace used by British kings.

The beautiful English countryside spread out on either side of the river. Children lined the bank, fishing or sailing small boats in the stream. Here and there, groups of picnickers relaxed in the sunshine on the grassy banks.

"The swans are the loveliest of all," Nan said, as the boat passed several of the majestic white birds.

Freddie and Flossie amused themselves by dangling their hands in the water over the side of the boat. All at once the little girl cried out, "Look, Nan! Isn't that a mother swan sitting over there?" She pointed to an extra large white bird sitting on her nest among the rushes at the water's edge.

"Yes, it is," Nan answered. She called to the pilot, "Will you please steer close to that swan so I can get a picture?" She took the camera from its case, careful not to disturb the miniature chair which was safely tucked in alongside of it.

"Righto," Tom said. Then he advised, "Go easy, me lass. When a swan gets 'is feelin's 'urt, 'e's apt to take a nip at your 'ead."

Tom cut the motor, and the boat drifted toward the big swan. With the air of a queen on her throne, she turned a haughty eye upon the oncoming Bobbseys. Soon the boat was within six or

seven feet of the swan. Nan raised the camera to
her eye.

Click!

The noise seemed to startle the mother swan.
She hissed and glared. Then Bert said, "Oh, oh,
look what's coming!"

From out in the river came a male swan, has-
tening to defend his mate and his home.

"Will—will he hurt us, Tom?" Flossie asked.

The man smiled, then said, "Not if you bribe
'im with a crust o' bread."

He added that he kept a bag of crusts for just
such an occasion. He handed a piece to Flossie.
She broke it into tiny pieces, and as the daddy
swan glided up, she threw him some bits.

Arching his long neck, the swan ate the bread.
This seemed to satisfy him, for he turned about
and swam off again into the middle of the river.

This gave Nan time to take some more pictures. The mother swan seemed to be used to the
twins by now. Instead of hissing, she ruffled her
feathers, stretched herself and rose, revealing
six large eggs lying in the nest.

"Oh-oh-oh!" Flossie exclaimed in surprise.
"Aren't they bee-yoo-ti-ful?"

All at once the mother swan placed her beak
under one of the eggs and flipped it over.

This time Flossie wailed, "Make her stop!
She's hurting her babies!"

CHAPTER XV

YOUNG KNIGHTS

"DON'T worry, Flossie. The swan is not hurting the eggs," Mrs. Bobbsey assured her small daughter.

She explained that this was what all setting birds do. "Watch!" she said.

As the motorboat drifted past the nest, the beautiful white bird flipped the remaining eggs with her bill, then fluttered down over them again. "She's now going to warm up the other side of the eggs," said Mrs. Bobbsey. "Someday they'll hatch out into baby cygnets."

Bert grinned. "Well baked on all sides," he joked.

The twins saw more swans and cygnets as they continued downriver toward Hampton Court. Finally the palace loomed up on the left shore. Unlike Windsor, Hampton Court had no towers.

Mrs. Bobbsey paid the riverman as the family

debarked at a dock close to the palace grounds. "It was a lovely trip," she told him.

"Good-by," Tom said, touching his cap and grinning. "I 'ope you enjoy 'Ampton Court. It's one o' me favorite spots in all o' merry ol' England."

A short while later the twins could see why this was so. A beautiful rectangular building was flanked with enormous green lawns and flower gardens.

Mrs. Bobbsey told them the palace had been built by Cardinal Wolsey. Later it had been a gift to King Henry the Eighth.

After wandering about the garden paths, the Bobbseys came to a high hedge. A sign at the entrance read: THE MAZE.

"Just like you built on Blueberry Island, Bert!" his twin said. "Oh, let's go in this one."

Mrs. Bobbsey laughed. "All right, but I hope we get out in time so we won't keep your father waiting. We'll stay together."

What fun and worries they had, as they twisted and turned along the boxwood paths! But they managed to figure out the right route and reached the exit.

Just then two boys ran past, shouting to each other. "Wait for me, Tim," one of them called.

"All right, Billy, but hurry."

From their voices, Bert thought they might be

Americans. "Hey, fellows, are you from the States?" he asked.

The boys stopped and turned around. Tim, about Bert's age, grinned. "We're Canadians," he said. "Our last name's Halsey." He introduced his brother Billy, who was six.

"We're on our way to the place where the knights used to joust," Tim said. "How about you fellows coming along?"

This sounded exciting to the Bobbsey boys. "May we go with them, Mother?" Bert asked.

"All right," she said. "We'll meet you here by the Maze. Don't be long."

The boys started off, their minds filled with visions of knights on horseback dashing at one another with long lances. Tim stopped when they reached a vast parking lot on the north side of the palace. At the moment there were not many cars in it.

"This was the jousting place," Tim said.

"You know a lot about Hampton Court," Freddie observed.

Tim said he had studied about Hampton Court in his Canadian school. "King Henry was a great sportsman," he told Bert and Freddie. "He had bowling on the green, tennis courts, archery ranges, and this jousting field."

"Boy, I'd like to have been a knight!" Freddie declared.

"I would, too," Billy chimed in.

Suddenly Freddie's eyes lighted up. "Why don't we play knight?" he proposed.

"How?" Billy wanted to know.

"Bert and Tim could be the horses. We'll be the riders."

"Great idea."

"How about it, Bert and Tim?" Freddie asked.

"Sure," both boys answered. "Climb on."

"There's only one trouble," said Billy. "We haven't any spears."

"We don't need them," Bert replied. "When you fellows get on our backs we'll dash toward each other. You knights can try to throw each other off."

Bert leaned over until his hands touched the ground, then Freddie sprang onto his brother's shoulders in pickaback fashion. Billy did the same with Tim, who pranced about like a frisky colt.

"Whoa!" cried Billy.

The older boys agreed to start toward each other from twenty paces apart. When Bert and Tim had taken their places, the Canadian boy cried out:

"Charge!"

The "horses" galloped toward each other, with Freddie and Billy yipping like Western cowboys. Passing Billy speedily, Freddie tried to grab him, but both riders slipped past without being dragged off.

Several sightseers, meanwhile, had stopped to look at the performance. They were laughing heartily.

The knights went back to the starting "posts," and Bert called out, "Charge!"

The boys raced toward each other for the second time. As they met, both Freddie and Billy flung their arms about the other, and each wrestled to throw his opponent.

Bert and Tim meanwhile were having a hard time keeping their balance. They wobbled back and forth as the younger boys pulled and tugged.

Then, at the same moment, Freddie and Billy unseated each other. With arms and feet flying wildly, both boys fell from their chargers!

"Ouch!" Freddie cried out, bumping his head on the ground.

"I guess the joust is a draw," said Bert. "Freddie and Billy are both winners!"

The little fellows grinned, but Freddie had clapped a hand to his forehead, which was bleeding.

In the meantime Mrs. Bobbsey, Nan, and Flossie had walked about a beautiful fountain on the opposite side of the palace.

"We'd better find the boys now," the twins'

mother said, and they started for the Maze.
When they arrived, Bert and Freddie were
not in sight. At this instant the attention of Mrs.
Bobbsey and the two girls was attracted by a bab-
ble of voices to the parking area.

Nan ran to investigate, then called back to her
mother, "There's a big crowd gathered over
here. I'm going to see why."

Mrs. Bobbsey and Flossie followed Nan, who
was first to reach the scene.

"Mother, come quickly!" Nan cried out. "It's Freddie!"

In the middle of a circle of onlookers stood the four boys who had played knight. A woman was opening a small first-aid kit.

"Here, lad," she said. "It's not much of an injury. I'll fix it in a minute." She put a small bandage on Freddie's forehead. "There," she added, "the knight has his badge of honor!"

"Well, Tim," Bert said, "I guess we'll have to go. If you ever come to Lakeport, look us up." The boys shook hands and said good-by.

Mrs. Bobbsey thanked the kind woman for her assistance. Then she and the twins hurried toward the main gate where they were to meet Mr. Bobbsey.

"There he is. I see him!" Freddie called, dashing on ahead of the others. Mr. Bobbsey was standing beside his car, waiting for them.

"What happened to you, Freddie?" he asked, noticing the bandage.

Freddie proudly told about the joust. His father said, smiling, "Maybe I can make you a Knight of the Round Table like the ones in King Arthur's court. That is, if we can find a restaurant with a round table."

The other Bobbseys laughed and confessed to being very hungry. They found a cheerful little restaurant on the street near by. The family had nearly finished eating their sandwiches when a man wearing an attendant's uniform came in and looked about.

"Mr. Bobbsey!" he called. "Paging Mr. Bobbsey."

The twins' father rose and introduced himself.

"I have a message for you," the attendant said, adding that he was from the Palace office. "Your hotel manager, sir, rang up our office and asked us to find you if possible. You are urgently wanted back in London."

"Did they say why?" Mr. Bobbsey asked worriedly.

"No, but the manager said for you to make haste."

Mr. Bobbsey thanked the attendant, who said, "Glad to be of service, sir," and walked off.

"Goodness, I wonder what has happened," Mrs. Bobbsey said.

"And how did the attendant know where to find you, Dad?" Bert asked.

Mr. Bobbsey said the hotel knew about the rented car and had probably suggested that the attendant try to spot it. Finding the car, he had figured they were in a nearby restaurant. "Let's go!" he urged.

The drive toward London led them through another park adjacent to the palace. On both sides of the road roamed herds of tame deer. There were no fences.

"These are smart deer," Bert said. "They seem to know enough to stay off the road."

Just then Freddie took an imaginary aim with an imaginary gun. "I see a rhino," he said. "Bang, bang!"

"You're shooting at a deer. Shame on you!" said Flossie.

Freddie replied that it was a pretend rifle. He could pretend to shoot anything he wanted to.

The boy took imaginary aim again. This time, however, there was a terrible *bang* beneath the car, and the Bobbseys' auto swayed to one side of the road!

CHAPTER XVI

RANSACKED!

AFTER recovering from the shock of the loud report, the Bobbseys felt the right rear wheel going *bump, bump, bump.*

"Oh, oh," Bert said, "we have a flat tire."

Mr. Bobbsey frowned. "I'd much rather that bang was from Freddie's imaginary gun."

Everyone alighted from the car. Bert helped his father jack up the rear and remove the wheel.

Meanwhile, Mrs. Bobbsey and the three other children walked into the park. They sat down in the shade of a chestnut tree which was in full blossom.

"I hope Bert and Daddy can change the tire quickly," Nan said anxiously. "Mother, I have a hunch something happened in our hotel room."

"We have nothing there of great value," Mrs. Bobbsey said.

158

"Oh, yes, we have," Nan reminded her. "Dad took the miniature throne room furniture back last night. Remember?"

"That's true," her mother admitted.

Just then the Bobbseys heard a dog barking in the distance. At the same time a small deer ran toward them as if trying to seek a safe place. The fawn came so close to Nan that she put her arm out and circled its neck. The small animal was shivering with fright.

The Bobbseys saw the reason for it a moment later. A large dog came bounding toward the tree.

"Go away!" Flossie called out.

"Shoo!" Mrs. Bobbsey said sharply as the dog began to circle the tree.

"Bert! Daddy! Help!" Flossie cried out.

Mr. Bobbsey and Bert heard the shout. Dropping their tools, they ran toward the others.

At once Bert said, "I don't think he's a bad dog." Getting closer to the animal, he called, "Here, boy! Come over here!"

Just then other shouts were heard in the deer park. The Bobbseys turned to see a woman and a girl about Nan's age running toward them.

"Buzz, come here! You naughty dog!" the girl cried out.

The dog immediately turned and leaped toward the little girl. She put a leash on him.

"Buzz jumped out of our car window when he saw the deer," the girl's mother said. "We're very sorry to have bothered you."

The fawn still shivered in Nan's arms as the woman and her daughter hurried off with their pet.

"You're all right now," Nan said, releasing the fawn. They watched smiling as it scampered off.

"Everything seems to be delaying our return to London," Mr. Bobbsey said impatiently as he and Bert returned to the car.

But in a few minutes the new tire was firmly in place. Bert put the tools away.

"All aboard, everybody!" Mrs. Bobbsey called out.

Half an hour later the car stopped in front of the Park Hotel. Mr. Bobbsey handed the doorman the car keys. "We're in a hurry," he said. "Will you please take care of the car for me, Archie?"

"Righto, sir."

The Bobbseys went directly to the manager's desk. "Oh, there you are, sir," he addressed Mr. Bobbsey. "We've been waiting for you. I'm afraid the news isn't good."

"What has happened?"

"Your suite has been ransacked."

"Ransacked!" Nan cried out.

The manager accompanied the Americans to the lift and hastened to their rooms with them.

"Oh dear!" Nan said as they stepped inside.

"What a mess!" Bert exclaimed.

Clothes and other articles were strewn about the floor. Chairs were overturned and ripped. Mattresses had been pulled from the beds.

"Have you any idea who did this?" Mr. Bobbsey asked the manager.

"We don't know, sir," came the reply. "The only stranger who came up in the lift, according to the operator, was a well-dressed man with a black beard."

"Silver Smitty!" Freddie declared.

"He's probably right," Bert said, and briefly told the manager about their unpleasant experiences with the thief.

Mrs. Bobbsey already was putting things in order and searching to see whether any of their property had been stolen.

"All of Mr. Bobbsey's and my possessions seem to be here," she told the manager.

"Well, perhaps the thief got into the wrong suite," he said, "and took nothing at all."

Nan, meanwhile, had asked her father where he had put the miniature furniture purchased at Windsor.

"In your top bureau drawer," he replied.

Nan raced into her room. The top bureau

drawer was upside down on the floor, along with clothes from the other drawers. Nan got down on her hands and knees and began rummaging through them.

Suddenly Nan cried out in alarm, "Daddy! Mother! The throne set—part of it's gone!"

The others hurried in. "All of it?" Mrs. Bobbsey asked.

"No. The throne and the crowns and the sceptre are here. But the three high-backed chairs are missing."

"Oh dear," Flossie wailed. "Now the doll queen's attendants won't have any place to sit down."

The hotel manager was very much embarrassed to learn that the miniature chairs were missing, especially since they were English articles purchased at Windsor.

"The hotel will have new ones made to your order," he said. "Can you describe them?"

"Why, yes. I have one. Oh, wait a minute!" Nan exclaimed suddenly.

Nan now recalled that the fourth little chair was packed in the camera case. And she had left it in the car parked in front of the hotel.

"I'll be right back," the girl said. She dashed from the room, just as two policemen arrived to take notes on the case.

Nan hurried to the lift, went to the lobby and

rushed out to the curb. The doorman was standing there, but the Bobbseys' car was gone!

"Oh!" Nan said, clapping a hand to her mouth in amazement. "Our car—it has been stolen!"

Noticing Nan's consternation, Archie hurried toward her. "Aren't you one of the Bobbseys?" he asked.

When Nan said yes, the man smiled. "Don't worry about your car," he said. "I moved it a little way down the street to a better parking spot."

Nan sighed in relief. "Oh, thank you," she said. "I was so worried." Then she added, "Did you see my camera case in the car when you moved it?"

The doorman said no, but it was probably safe. He had been watching the car.

Nan scooted down the street. The fright had made her tremble a little. "Oh, don't be such a ninny!" she told herself.

But as she neared the parked auto, Nan again cried out in alarm. A man with a thin face and blond hair had opened the rear door on the right side of the automobile.

As Nan approached on the sidewalk, the fellow was groping about inside, as if looking for something. Suddenly Nan saw his long, bony hand come to rest on the camera case. The fellow pulled it out of the car and slammed the door.

"Stop! That's mine!" Nan shouted at him.

"I say, what's going on there?" Archie called, hearing the commotion.

"A thief is stealing my camera!" Nan shrieked.

As the doorman came running, the intruder dashed past several more parked cars, then he took to the sidewalk.

"Stop! Come back with my camera!" Nan cried as she and Archie raced after the fellow.

Several passers-by, hearing the warning, tried to grab the fugitive. One man got his hands on the fellow's coat, but the blond-haired thief squirmed out of his grip and raced down a side alley. Nan and the doorman were in hot pursuit.

"If only a bobby would show up to block his path!" Nan hoped fervently. But there was not a policeman in sight.

The alley led into a cobblestoned square lined with small shops. Many people were hurrying about.

"Catch that thief! Oh, please catch that thief!" Nan cried breathlessly, as the man disappeared among the crowd of shoppers.

CHAPTER XVII

HIDDEN WRITING

FOR a moment Nan thought that the thief surely would be caught this time. As he hastened past a woman, she dropped her bag of greens and seized the man by a coat lapel. But he pushed her roughly aside and jumped through the doorway of a small sandwich shop.

Nan dashed in after him, with Archie close at her heels. The thief raced to the back of the small restaurant, then down the basement steps.

In her haste to follow Nan bumped squarely against a table at which a man was drinking tea. His cup teetered, sloshing the tea into his lap.

"I say, what ails you?" he called out angrily.

"Oh, I'm so sorry," Nan said, stopping to apologize. "But I'm chasing a thief who stole my camera!"

The few seconds' delay was enough to give the fugitive a good lead. Nan and Archie descended the stairway into a dark cellar, then saw a crack of light which came from a door leading to a rear alleyway. The girl flung the door open, climbed a few stone steps and found herself in a narrow passageway between two buildings.

"Oh, where did that thief go?" Nan wailed, as Archie came puffing after her.

Behind him was Bert, who explained that he had gone downstairs to join his sister. He had arrived in front of the hotel in time to see Nan and the doorman dash around the corner.

"Oh dear!" Nan wailed. "We had such wonderful pictures in the camera. And the fourth miniature chair, too."

"Let's look around here," Bert suggested. "Maybe the fellow got scared and dropped the camera."

Nan was not very hopeful of finding it, but she helped Bert and Archie search.

Suddenly Bert called out, "Look! I've found it!"

Pushing a trash container to one side, the boy picked up the case. The zipper was open. Inside was the camera and some film.

But the miniature chair was missing!

"Nan, this whole mystery has something to do with those four chairs," Bert declared.

"But what would make them so valuable?" Nan puzzled.

Sadly the twins walked back to their hotel. Archie said he was sorry about what had happened and he would report it to the police immediately.

"They are upstairs in our rooms now," Bert said. "We'll tell them."

As the twins were about to enter the hotel, they heard someone calling them from across the street. Turning quickly, they saw Gail and Gavin Radford coming out of Green Park.

"Bert! Nan! Wait for us! We have something to show you!" Gavin called out.

The brother and sister crossed the street carefully in the swift-moving traffic. Bert and Nan noticed that Gavin held something in his hands.

"We thought you'd like these," Gavin said.

The twins gasped in amazement. In the boy's hand were three of the miniature chairs! But how different they looked now! The tapestry cushions had been slashed with a knife, and the stuffing stuck out helter-skelter.

"Where did you get these?" Nan cried, tears coming to her eyes.

"In the park underneath a bench," Gail said.

The English children reported that they had seen the miniatures while waiting in Green Park for the Bobbseys to return to their hotel.

"We thought perhaps you'd like to repair them for your collection," Gavin said.

"Why these are chairs we bought and they were stolen from my room!" Nan said.

"What!" Gavin exclaimed.

Bert quickly told of the rapid series of events and Gavin whistled. "I say, that is a mystery!"

Bert suggested that they all return to the spot where the Radfords had found the miniatures. "Perhaps the thief dropped a clue of some sort."

Nan told the doorman where they were going.

He promised to report the theft of the fourth miniature chair to the policemen in the Bobbseys' rooms and hastened inside the hotel.

The four children crossed the street and ran through the park entrance. The bench where the slashed chairs had been found was not far from the spot where the Bobbseys had tried to trap the writer of the threatening note.

The twins and their friends searched the area. If they could only find some article which the culprit might have dropped!

Suddenly Nan came upon a scrap of folded white paper. "I wonder if this is anything," she said, opening it.

On the paper was written the Bobbseys' name and their hotel address!

"That's a good clue, eh?" Gavin exclaimed.

Bert said it was hard to get fingerprints from a piece of paper like this. But suddenly he had an idea. Holding the paper up to the light, he looked through it.

Nan looked through the paper also. On it she could see small indentations, as if a note had been written on the top sheet and the pencil had pressed through.

"Perhaps the police can help us," Bert said. He put the note into his pocket. Carrying the slashed miniature chairs, he and the others hastened back to the hotel. Gail and Gavin said they would remain in the lobby while Bert and Nan went upstairs.

The twins found the police still searching the ransacked apartment. The two officers were amazed to learn of the paper Nan had found. One of them, using the Bobbseys' magnifying glass, examined the sheet carefully.

"There is an address on here," he said. "No doubt it was written on the top sheet. It's in the Soho district."

"I think I know the reason for these thefts," Nan declared.

As the police and her family listened, she said that the thief must have been looking for something secreted inside the bottom of the tiny chairs.

"A good deduction," the hotel manager said. "The thief came to this room and stole the three chairs. Then he went into the park and cut them open, but did not find what he was looking for."

"Exactly," Bert spoke up. "Then the fellow searched our car and found the camera case. In it was the fourth miniature chair."

"Oh, if we could only stop that man from ripping it apart!" Nan said with a sigh.

"Perhaps we can," one of the policemen declared. He suggested some of them hasten to Soho. "I have a hunch we'll find the thief at this address."

It was decided that the two officers together with Mr. Bobbsey and the older twins would hurry to the mysterious address.

"We can use my car," Mr. Bobbsey said as they took the lift.

The five got in, and one of the bobbies took the wheel. He sped through the streets and soon arrived at a dwelling in a narrow lane. Houses and shops stood side by side.

"This isn't the smartest part of London," the driver remarked, as they all got out.

Nan thought that the brownstone house before which they stood was a spooky-looking place. Several windows on the first floor were boarded up. A rusted iron railing led down a flight of stone steps to a basement apartment.

"This house looks deserted," Mr. Bobbsey said.

Suddenly Bert detected a noise coming from the basement. "I think someone's down there," he whispered.

The officers motioned for silence. Then on tiptoes they descended the litter-covered steps to the basement door.

The Bobbseys could hear a sudden thud as the officers flung themselves against the door, which flew wide open. Then with hearts pounding, the twins heard the stern command:

"You're under arrest! Stand where you are!"

CHAPTER XVIII

THE TOWER SECRET

A MOMENT later, the officers called the Bobbseys to the basement. They entered a dingy room, lighted only by a small bulb in a dusty yellow-shaded lamp.

As Bert's eyes became accustomed to the gloom, he noticed that the prisoner was the same sour-faced man who had plagued the Bobbseys since their arrival in London.

"He's the one who's been bothering us!" the boy cried out.

"And stole our camera case with the miniature chair in it," Nan declared.

The prisoner, who said his name was Guy Nero, at first denied that he was guilty. "I tell you I didn't do a thing wrong," he said.

The policemen started to search the prisoner. At the same time the Bobbseys looked carefully about the sparsely furnished room. Bert and

Nan pulled out a rickety sofa and looked behind it.

In a pile of dust stood the miniature chair!

"Oh!" Nan exclaimed, bending down to pick it up. "It's ripped to pieces just like the others."

At that moment one of the officers, who had been searching the prisoner's shoes, cried out, "I say, what's this?" From Guy Nero's shoe he pulled a tiny roll of black film.

"That must be what he found in the chair cushion," Nan deduced.

She handed the policeman the chair. He compared the size of the torn seat with the roll of film. It fitted perfectly into the jagged hole!

"So that's why you stole the four little chairs," Mr. Bobbsey declared hotly.

"I didn't steal all of them," the prisoner blurted.

"Just this one, eh?" the bobby went on. "So you admit your guilt?"

Guy Nero looked glum. "All right," he said. "I did take this chair from the camera case, but not the others at the hotel." He stared first at the Bobbseys, then at the officers. "How did you know where to find me?"

"That's our secret," the policeman replied with a sidewise wink at Bert.

"I know," Guy Nero stormed angrily. "Silver Smitty tipped you off to where I was."

"What if he did?" the officer asked, as he unrolled the black piece of film and held it toward the lamp light.

"That's microfilm," Mr. Bobbsey spoke up.

"Righto."

Now the prisoner thrashed about frantically as the second policeman grasped his arm tightly. "Don't try to get away. You haven't a chance."

"Okay," Nero hissed. "I'll tell you about it, but don't put all the blame on me."

As the others listened, the thief said that Silver Smitty was the one who had ransacked the Bobbseys' hotel suite. He did this to find the microfilm concealed in one of the miniature chairs. But when he did not locate it, he had blamed Guy Nero for taking it.

"I was afraid of Smitty, so I thought I'd try myself to find the other chair and give it to him."

"How fortunate that he never had a chance to see Silver Smitty!" Nan thought.

The thief continued, "I figured the chair might still be in the Bobbseys' car. I was looking for it when you saw me. All I had time to grab was the camera case."

Nero readily admitted that the dingy room had been used as a hideout.

"That film must be very important," Bert said, "for those men to take so much trouble to find it."

The two officers took turns questioning, until Nero, perspiring, was exhausted from evading the truth.

"Stop! Stop!" he cried finally. "I'll tell you what it's all about. That microfilm contains plans of how to steal the crown jewels from the Tower of London."

"What!" the Bobbseys cried out.

"It would never have worked," Mr. Bobbsey said. "That place has every kind of protection."

Guy Nero, thoroughly dejected, fell back on the sofa. He blurted out the rest of the story.

The plans for the robbery had been worked out by a master thief in prison. But he had died there. However, a buddy, who was leaving, had put the plans on microfilm when he got out. Then he had hidden it in a chair of the miniature throne room furniture which he had stolen.

"He was waiting for Silver Smitty to come and help him with the robbery. But in the meantime some bloke sold the set by mistake!

"Smitty and me tried everywhere to find it," Guy Nero went on. "He even went to the States and ransacked a store in Lakeport run by an Englishman."

"Mr. Warwick's shop!" Nan cried.

"But why did he take the miniature TV set and the silver?" Bert asked.

Guy Nero declared that Silver Smitty could

not resist taking silver whenever he saw it, particularly small, valuable pieces. He figured the little TV set was something special.

"That proved his undoing," Mr. Bobbsey said, proudly putting an arm around Bert and Nan.

Silver Smitty, his pal declared, had crossed the Atlantic on the *Ocean Princess*. A friend, working in the kitchen crew, had helped the thief hide on board.

"We arrested that fellow this morning," one officer said. "But we were keeping it quiet until the proper time."

"It doesn't matter now," Guy Nero said. "The whole plan was wrecked by this American detective and his children." He pointed weakly at Mr. Bobbsey.

"I'm not a detective. I'm a lumberman," Mr. Bobbsey said.

Guy Nero looked amazed. He declared that Silver Smitty and his friends thought Mr. Bobbsey was posing as a lumberman and really was a detective!

"My twins are the detectives," Mr. Bobbsey said, smiling.

Guy Nero groaned at hearing this, saying that Silver Smitty's great mistake was to have gone anywhere near Lakeport.

The rest of the story was quickly told. After Silver Smitty had escaped from the *Ocean Prin-*

cess with the oilskin sack, he made his way directly to the hideout. While there he heard rumors that the microfilm had been tied under a wing of Old Blackie, the raven at the Tower of London.

Smitty and Nero had kidnapped the bird and escaped with him in a car. But when they had tried to examine the raven, Old Blackie had pecked Smitty on the cheek, then fluttered out the window and got lost near Trafalgar Square.

The day the Bobbseys had visited the monument, Guy Nero was there searching for the raven. "But you had him."

"And you couldn't take him away from my dad," Bert said proudly.

Nero had reported back to Smitty. "We decided you Bobbseys had the microfilm," he said. "But some of our friends thought that you knew where the throne room set was and had gone to Windsor to buy it."

Nero admitted he had tried to get the Bobbsey twins to the cheap store and force them to tell what they knew. But the plan had not worked because Bert had spotted Mr. Warwick's miniature TV set there.

"That just about clears up the mystery, doesn't it?" Mr. Bobbsey declared, as the officers shoved Nero toward the door.

"Where is Silver Smitty now?" the officer

asked, as he led the thief up the steps to the street.

"Probably at the Tower of London trying to work out his own plan to steal the jewels. He said he was going to go there today."

One officer asked the other policeman to telephone for a car to take Guy Nero to jail. He himself hopped into Mr. Bobbsey's auto with the twins and their father.

"We're going to the Tower of London," he said.

Arriving there, the officer said, "We'll walk around slowly so as not to attract attention. The minute you identify this Silver Smitty, let me know."

Bert and Nan felt their hearts pounding. Inside the Tower grounds scores of sightseers wandered about, unaware of the search for the clever thief.

"Where do you suppose he is?" Bert whispered.

Nan thought the most likely place would be at the display of crown jewels.

"Then let's go there," Bert urged.

Hurrying on ahead of Mr. Bobbsey and the officer, they paid their fee and climbed up into the stone tower. A crowd of visitors milled about the sparkling display. Bert and Nan looked from face to face.

"I doubt if he'll be wearing the same beard here," Nan said in a low voice to Bert.

"The minute you identify this Silver Smitty, let me know."

Just then Bert stopped short. Bending close to Nan, he said, "Look at the fellow over there. He has a mark on his cheek. Probably where Old Blackie nipped him. And he moves and walks like Silver Smitty."

Before making any outcry, Bert and Nan watched the man closely. He seemed to be studying the huge glass-enclosed exhibit. Every now and then he paused to make a sketch on a pad he held in his hand. He was so intent upon what he was doing that he did not notice the Bobbsey twins moving up behind him.

Not far from them were their father and the policeman. Bert raised his right hand to beckon to the officer. He came over quickly.

"This is the man," Bert said quietly.

What happened surprised the Bobbseys. The officer made no fuss at all. First he alerted several Beefeaters who stood near by, directing the sightseers. Then he moved in beside the suspect. In a low voice he said: "Come with me."

The man gave a start, his cruel eyes glancing about for a route of escape. Seeing none, he went quietly with the policeman while other Beefeaters surrounded him. The tourists were not aware of what was happening.

When they were all outside in the courtyard, the man said defiantly, "What do you want with me? I haven't broken any law."

"You're Silver Smitty," Bert accused him.

At that moment a detail of policemen hurried up to the group. The sergeant in charge quickly identified Silver Smitty from prison pictures. He was marched off.

He turned for a moment, however, to shake a fist at the Bobbseys. "You're too smart!" he snarled.

After the captive had gone, the Beefeater who had posed for the Bobbseys' pictures came up to congratulate them. "We are grateful to you," he said and shook their hands. "An attempted robbery here is a most unpleasant thing to handle."

News of Silver Smitty's arrest and the capture of certain friends appeared in the London newspapers the next day. And near evening the hotel manager knocked at the door of the Bobbseys' suite.

"We are having a surprise party for the Bobbsey twins and their parents," he said, and escorted them to the dining room.

"How exciting!" said Nan.

To greet the Bobbseys were a police official, the Radford family, and even Tim and Billy. The children had heard about the Bobbseys' success and had come to the hotel to see their friends.

The hotel manager seated the guests at a long table. What a gala party it was, with everyone talking and laughing at once! The delicious dinner wound up with Freddie's and Flossie's favorite, banana pretties.

"We never thought we'd solve this kind of a mystery when we came to London," Bert said.

"We're glad you came," the police official said as he chatted with Mr. Bobbsey. Then he stood up and made a short speech. After praising the children again, he said, "And now I have a surprise for you Americans."

He handed Bert a white envelope bearing the seal of the City of London.

The boy arose and opened it. As he read, a grin came over his face. "This is great," he said.

"What does it say?" Flossie asked.

Bert read it aloud:

"In appreciation of the fine work of the Bobbsey twins, the City of London has granted them a lifetime pass to the Tower of London."

The guests gave a rousing cheer. Even Cedric, the stuffed raven, looking across the room from his perch, seemed to smile at the good news.